Why You Shouldn't Throw a Snake at Your Mother

To my dear cousin Robin

Phil

Why You Shouldn't Throw a Snake at Your Mother

A Novel

Phil Gray

iUniverse, Inc.
New York Lincoln Shanghai

Why You Shouldn't Throw a Snake at Your Mother

Copyright © 2007 by Phil Gray

All rights reserved. No part of this book may be used or reproduced by any means, graphic, electronic, or mechanical, including photocopying, recording, taping or by any information storage retrieval system without the written permission of the publisher except in the case of brief quotations embodied in critical articles and reviews.

iUniverse books may be ordered through booksellers or by contacting:

iUniverse
2021 Pine Lake Road, Suite 100
Lincoln, NE 68512
www.iuniverse.com
1-800-Authors (1-800-288-4677)

Because of the dynamic nature of the Internet, any Web addresses or links contained in this book may have changed since publication and may no longer be valid.

This is a work of fiction. All of the characters, names, incidents, organizations, and dialogue in this novel are either the products of the author's imagination or are used fictitiously.

ISBN: 978-0-595-44810-4 (pbk)
ISBN: 978-0-595-89129-0 (ebk)

Printed in the United States of America

For Donna Mae, my love, my life.

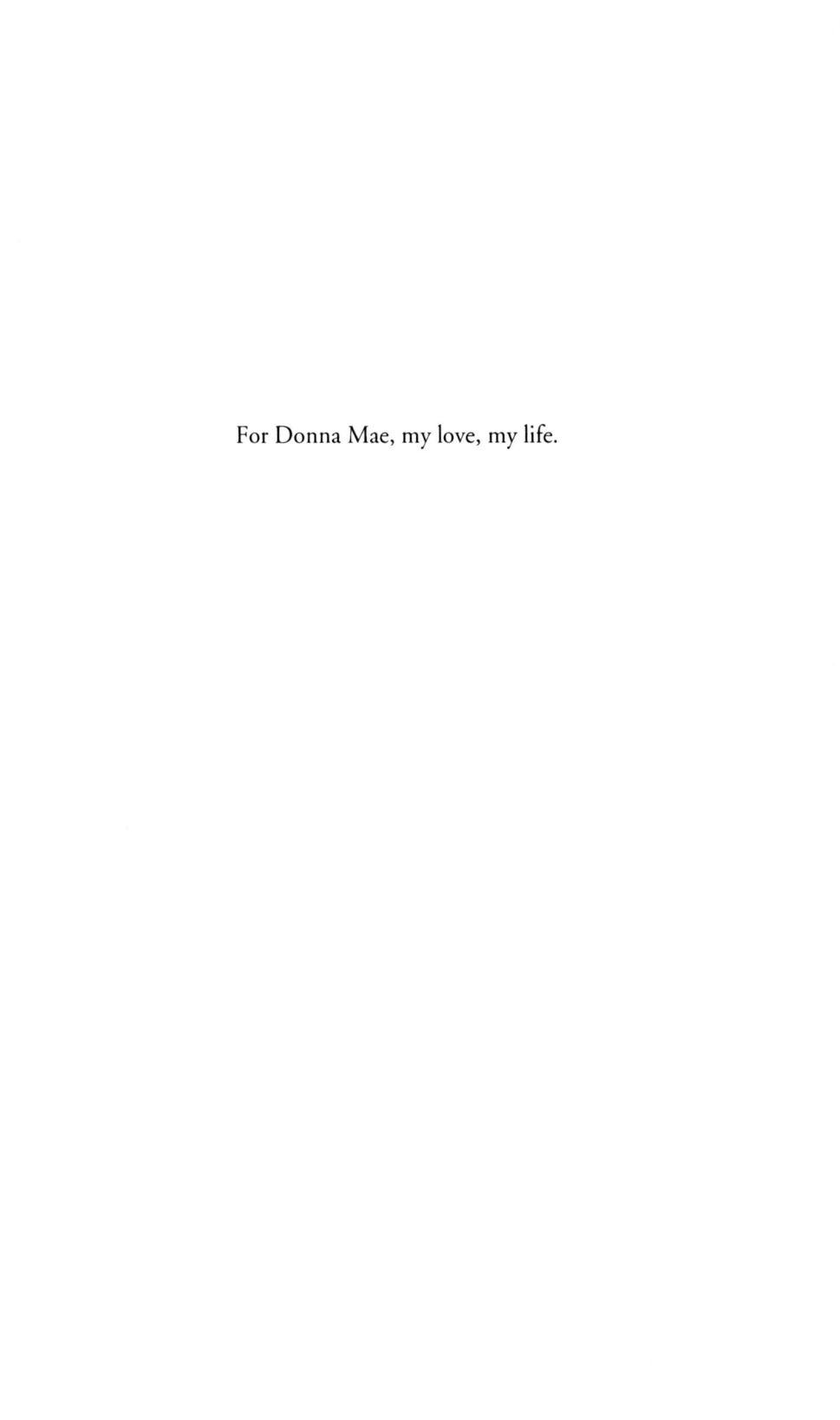

1

IT WAS COMMON KNOWLEDGE that the Woods behind my house in Milford, Connecticut were teeming with the most venomous of vipers. Everybody knew that. Charlie Miller, Pudgy Tookis, and I knew that because two big kids told us. These were neighborhood big kids, twelve-year-olds, who already had hair on their legs; we were only ten, and had none, so naturally we believed every word they said.

"You can't imagine the snakes in them woods! Fat, monstrous Copperheads, thousands of 'em, big around as your arm, lurking behind every rock and tree," said Big Kid #1.

"Yeah, and hideous, slimy Water Moccasins, ten feet long, slithering through every creek and stream," added Big Kid #2.

"Big snakes. Angry snakes. Hungry snakes. Poisonous snakes. Killer snakes. All kinds of nasty-ass snakes. They got jaws can open wide as your head, and fangs like ice picks," said #1.

"You can't hardly walk in there without stepping on one," said #2.

"And if you do step on one, you're dead," said #1, "on accounta it'll jump right up onto your face. Snakes can jump that high, honest. They love ten-year-olds too, cuz you're short and easy to get to, and also because you're young and soft and taste juicy."

"They don't bother us cuz we're big; they hafta work too hard to get to us. We don't taste good like you guys either. That's why we can play there," said #2.

"I'd stay outa there if I was you," said #1, putting the finishing touch on their fabrication.

They made it sound like all the snakes in the world were banded together, right there in our Woods, in an insidious reptilian conspiracy dedicated to the elimination of ten-year-olds from the face of the earth. This may seem far-fetched to adults, but to us, it made perfect sense.

And it was made all the more believable by the dark and sinister nature of the Woods themselves—to us a veritable forest primeval. Leggy vines dangled to the ground from high in tall trees, whose canopies caused perpetual shade, encouraging ferns and lichens to cover the ground kept moist by underground tidal forces that inhibited natural drainage. Large trees, blown over by hurricanes, lay on their side, exposing huge root balls the size of a Packard. Pools of murky water filled large cavities where the root balls had been, providing drinking water for raccoons and handy lairs for snakes. Weeds, bushes, and smaller trees filled in between the larger trees, making passage difficult for intrepid kids and ideal for slithering serpents. Farther in, towards the beach, low-lying wetlands gave birth to reeds and cattails, growing tall and dense in swampy mire, making passage undesirable for hardy naturalists and ideal for slithering serpents. Random sounds, mostly hushed—birds flapping, toads croaking, rodents scurrying—checked the otherwise eerie quiet, gave the bravest intruder chicken skin.

Our neighborhood had been developed on the solid ground surrounding this area of woodlands and marsh so obviously unsuitable for human habitation and so primly avoided by the citizenry that it was known famously as the "Woods."

Everything about the Woods was adverse to humans and ideal for snakes.

Charlie, Pudgy and I were eternally grateful to the two big kids for warning us of the dangers in the Woods. Never mind that they stretched the facts a bit, claiming that Copperheads and Water Moccasins ranged as far north as Connecticut. We took their intelligence at face value. After all, big kids knew such things—especially these big kids, because they *played* in the Woods. Egad, can you imagine: they played in the Woods as fearlessly as we played in our own yard. What balls!

We were in blind awe of the big kids' courage, innocently unaware that their tales were laced with every embellishment and bold-face lie the wisdom of twelve years could manufacture. Their intention was not malicious, you see. No, not at all! Big kids own their woods. They were simply protecting a sovereign right.

If you are twelve years old, you simply cannot have ten-year-olds running amuck on your sacred turf.

The Big Kids' scare-tactics worked to perfection that summer long ago. Charlie Miller, Pudgy Tookis, and I were scared to death—of the Woods in general, and of snakes in particular. What should have been a cautious childhood fascination with reptiles became a consuming paranoia. Our parents could not assuage our fear; they didn't *know anything about the Woods*. How could they? They didn't *play in the Woods*, so they couldn't possibly fathom the danger there.

2

THIS WAS THE SUMMER OF 1952. Baseball was in the air in America, the Summer Olympics were underway in Finland, and a nasty war was sputtering in Korea. Our world was largely unaffected by these events. School was out, and we were at play … everywhere except, of course, in the Woods.

The year had started with a yawn—Dimitri Shostakovich finishing his fifth string quartet, the Dutch finishing a new Bible translation, Elizabeth Taylor marrying Michael Wilding a second time—and didn't get the first jolt of consequence until the end of February when Winston Churchill announced Britain's first atomic bomb.

After that, things picked up. Puerto Rico became a self-governing U.S. commonwealth, the Communists re-invigorated their offensive in Korea, the U.S. Senate finally ratified the peace treaty restoring sovereignty to Japan, and the most important contribution to the pop culture of the civilized world, the very first Rock and Roll concert, called the *Moondog Coronation Ball*, was introduced at the Cleveland Arena by a local disc jockey named Alan Freed—peace be upon him.

The Jackie Gleason Show, featuring the *Honeymooners*, debuted on television that year. Earnest Hemingway published *The Old Man and the Sea*, and William Gaines published the first *Mad* comic book. Herman Wouk won a Pulitzer Prize for *Caine Mutiny*, and Humphrey Bogart received the Academy Award for Best Actor in the 1951 movie *African Queen*. The Academy Award for best 1951 film went to *An American in Paris*. The big 1952 movie hits were *High Noon*, *The Greatest Show on Earth*, and *Moulin Rouge*.

In the Summer Olympics, Emil Zatopec, from Czechoslovakia, won the 5,000 meters, the 10,000 meters, *and* the Marathon, the latter a race he had never run before. Imagine Emil's conversation with his coach before the marathon: "Ya know, Coach, the 5K and 10K were pretty wimpy races; I feel like running a marathon. Whaddya think?" Coach: "You oughta have your head examined."

There was a correct alignment of planets and stars for the World Series; the New York Yankees beat the Brooklyn Dodgers. The legends who played in those games were household names. Some still are. For the Yankees: Hank Bauer, Yogi Berra, Mickey Mantle, Gil McDougald, Allie Reynolds, and Phil Rizzuto. For the Dodgers: Roy Campanella, Billy Cox, Carl Erskine, Gil Hodges, Pee Wee Reese, and Jackie Robinson. Anyone who didn't follow the World Series that year lived under a rock.

In the presidential race, Dwight David Eisenhower was elected to succeed Harry Truman. Richard Nixon became the new Vice President.

Overseas, George VI of England died and his eldest daughter became Elizabeth II. Egypt's King Farouk was ousted by a military coup. Greece and Turkey joined a NATO that had just approved a European army.

While no one seemed to be paying attention, the U.S. tested its first hydrogen device on Enewetak Atoll in the South Pacific, and Jonas Salk developed the first Polio vaccine.

And while no one seemed to notice the gulf of irony between his search for truth and his racist view of black Africans, Albert Schweitzer won the Nobel Peace Prize for his philosophy called "reverence for life."

In business, BOAC began the first passenger jet service, with a flight from London to Rome, and we were all on our way to seeing the world.

In finance, Franklin National Bank in Long Island, New York issued the first bank credit card, and we were all on our way into debt seeing the world.

The population of the U.S. was 157.6 million.
The average life expectancy was 68.6 years.
The average house cost just under $17,000.
Candy bars cost a nickel.
A bottle of coke was a dime.
Gas was 20¢ a gallon.
A first-class postage stamp was 3¢.
The minimum wage was 75¢ per hour.

3

AND, OF COURSE, THERE WAS TELEVISION. Brand spanking new. In its birth throes. But despite the popularity of new forms of entertainment it spawned, such as *The Jackie Gleason Show* and Dave Garroway's *Today Show*, a television set was expensive and out of reach for most folks in small towns.

A typical set consisted of a small black and white screen the size of a dinner plate housed in a shiny wood cabinet the size of a refrigerator. The television signal was received either by an aerial on the roof or by a contraption known as "Rabbit Ears."

Rabbit Ears were two 18-inch metal prongs sticking up V-shape from a free-standing plastic base, usually placed atop the television set. Rabbit Ears were a pain in the neck because they had to be adjusted constantly to get good reception—meaning a proper image on the screen.

A typical roof aerial was a boxy cluster of aluminum prongs atop an aluminum mast. Most people strapped the mast to the chimney such that the cluster of prongs sat eight or ten feet above the peak of the house. The mast was secured with several guy wires attached to various points on the roof.

A roof aerial was more expensive than Rabbit Ears, but was preferred by most folks because it provided better reception. It could not, however, be adjusted from inside the house. On rare occasions, when high winds tweaked the orientation of the aerial, disrupting reception, the man-of-the-house—mothers were too smart to attempt this—hauled out the extension ladder, scrambled up on the roof on all fours like a monkey, manipulated the aerial's orientation, and shouted back and forth with the person inside the house appointed to watch the television screen and shout "enough," or some such, when reception was restored.

Our neighbors, the Jablonski's, three doors down, had the only television set in the neighborhood. They let a half-dozen of us kids watch *Howdy Doody* every night at 5:30 PM, provided we all sat on the floor.

I was more interested in the Jablonski's next-door neighbor, Peggy Flahrety, than I was in *Howdy Doody*. I tried on several occasions to put my arm around her as I'd seen the big kids do in the balcony at the movies, but she wouldn't let me, no matter how smoothly the execution. Ten-year-olds have notoriously short attention spans and I was living proof of that. After too many false starts, I lost interest in Peggy Flahrety and fell into watching the show.

The boss of the show was a human named Buffalo Bob, a perky fellow from upstate New York who had never seen a buffalo. He wore a brown leather-looking jacket with fringes hanging from the pockets and sleeves, smacking more of Liberace than Davy Crocket. Another human, Clarabelle the Clown, wore a proper clown outfit but didn't do proper clown tricks. He was cast mute, and communicated with honking sounds, reminiscent of Harpo Marx but not that funny. The rest of the characters were puppets, the most prominent of which was Howdy Doody, aptly named. An American Indian character, Princess Summerfall Winterspring, was originally a puppet, but was switched that year to a *live* woman, the most gorgeous live woman I had ever seen. This simple switch, in my opinion, saved the show from slipping into oblivion. And it caused me to experience my first mini-jolt of sexual excitement—Peggy Flahrety notwithstanding.

The show had an audience of sorts, the Peanut Gallery, a group of little kids huddled together behind a low railing. They were part of the show. From time to time, the camera wandered over to capture candid glimpses of their gleeful faces, as if to assure watching parents they were invitees not inmates. These little peanuts were within sniffing distance, or so it seemed, of the lovely Princess Summerfall Winterspring. "Aha!" I remember thinking, "now we're getting somewhere."

The Peanut Gallery became the preferred place to be in the whole world. I had dreams about it—involving the Princess rather, and awkward positions. I still have those dreams from time to time.

For countless hours, Charlie, Pudgy, and I fantasized about sitting in the front row of the Peanut Gallery, surreptitiously gauging the movements of Buffalo Bob and Clarabelle the Clown, so that, at just the right moment, when their backs were turned, we could spring across the railing and plant a big fat kiss on the lips of the Princess.

We had no idea how to go about getting into the Peanut Gallery. The concept was too abstract. We were more than a long way from any springing and kissing. The futility of the fantasy eventually won out, leaving us in a vacuum of emotions, into which returned the subject we had tried to keep hindmost in our thoughts that summer: snakes.

So by default, snakes took center stage.

4

I DO NOT ABIDE snakes. In fact, I hate snakes.

I have snake nightmares.

Show me a snake and I'll show you a 10-flat Hundred.

There is no such thing as a good snake.

It should be illegal to own one, or even touch one.

Holding a snake can make you go blind.

Snakes are slimy.

Snakes cause warts.

Snakes are proof there is no God.

If the Yankees had a snake for a mascot, I would root for the Dodgers (now *that*, is extreme).

If some fool brings a pet snake to school for show-and-tell, I'm home sick.

I don't go to zoos with snakes in cages—herpetariums, is that a word?—on the off chance that one might escape. Although, I'll admit, if there must be snakes on the planet, cages are the second-best place for them; set in concrete is the first-best.

I once saw an Australian chap, sitting on the sofa in his living room, fondling a snake like it's a kitten, saying, "What a beautiful snyke, she is." Christ, the guy's nuts! Imagine having a sleep-over at his house?

Worse yet, the rheumy-eyed snake-walla in India kissing cobras. Jeez! I'd rather kiss a hot rivet.

I can't even wear a snake-skin belt.

The truth is, I'm in the vast majority. Snakes are universally unpopular with just about everybody. Look at nursery rhymes, popular characters, and role models: Easter *Bunny*, Santa's *Reindeers*, *Groundhog* Day, Three Little *Pigs*, Mickey *Mouse*, Donald *Duck*, Smokey *Bear*, *Lassie*, *Trigger*, *Flipper*, and so on. All household names. There is even a lovable *crocodile*—of all things—in *Peter Pan*, but there is no lovable snake, no snake with a household name. For good reason.

If one digs deep enough, one might discover the python, Kaa, in Rudyard Kipling's *The Jungle Book*, and be inclined to say, "Aha! Kaa helped rescue Mowgli. He's good. There's a fine snake." And he may be that, to the extent there is such a thing as a fine snake. But if so, it's a bizarre exception. A python is *not* cuddly, is *not* friendly, is *certainly not* trainable, and is *not* preferred by most adults and all children. Don't take my word for it; ask any adult except Alice Cooper, or ask a kid.

Rudyard Kipling is a giant *among the giants* of English literature. He could give poignancy to a doorknob and morality to a tumor, but he could not popularize a snake, at least not for American consumption.

I make it a practice to stay as far away from snakes as possible. If I see one, my heart skips a beat and droplets of sweat form on my brow. If, by some sadistic turn of fate, for which I would surely be undeserving, I am ever bitten by a snake—any kind of snake—treat my heart first, then treat the snake bite.

Strangely enough, my fear of snakes merely *began* with the big kids' tales of the Woods. It was my very own dear mother who sealed the bargain. It happened that summer, as I will now relate.

5

THERE IS AN INSIDIOUS male curse—a curse of testosterone—that compels young boys, and grown men as well, to identify, face down, and conquer, a worst fear. It is an indiscriminate curse, and it strikes without warning.

I must have done something in an earlier life to earn a double dose of the curse. Or perhaps the curse, acting on its own initiative, just decided to visit me as a single dose but with a humorous twist. The net effect is the same. That's how the curse works. It is also impetuous and egalitarian. It has neither friend nor foe, just candidates—or victims, depending on your point of view.

One minute I was frolicking mindlessly, enjoying the summer, mooning over a beautiful princess, ogling a cute neighbor, oiling my baseball glove, swimming at the beach, happy as a clam and half as cognizant. The next minute I was struck dumb, the curse upon me. A conclusion burst into my head from nowhere, instantaneously like the Big Bang, fully formed, incontestable. There was no intermediate period of contemplation between the bursting and the forming, the conclusion just materialized, complete, ready for execution.

I would face down my worst fear; I would find a snake and hold it in my hand. But that's not all; that would be too simple. The double-dose requirement was that my performance be executed with a splash of bravado. With a snake in my hand, I would stand tall; I would wave it in the face of my peers to gain their fawning adulation; then I would take it home and throw it at my mother. She would freak.

"What a great gag!" I thought, my little brain deluding itself with the prospect of recognition and fame.

Charlie Miller and Pudgy Tookis were my best friends because they were perfect co-conspirators for a good prank. And this one, involving a non-lethal surprise attack upon a mother, was as good as a prank can be.

It would be incorrect to conclude from this story that I hated my mother. I did not, I loved my mother.
"Love is Strange"—Mickey and Sylvia.

6

CHARLIE MILLER WAS A RAGGED little urchin that *none* of the kids in the neighborhood were allowed to play with. That's because Charlie lived on another planet. He didn't seem to have any rules, or at least he wasn't aware that he did. He was a free spirit way before the '60s.

All Hail! It was the Charlie's of the world who invented the '60s.

I never saw Charlie clean, and I always knew what he had for lunch because he wore the remnants of it on the front of him like a badge of honor. To Charlie, meals were an adventure, his mouth was a target, and his hands were the shooters. Every afternoon after lunch, a shimmering rainbow of juices and food particles could be seen dripping from his chin, sluicing down his shirt, pants, and even to his shoes. Ordinarily, shoes don't draw flies, but Charlie's did.

He was tall for his age, and thin, almost to the point of emaciation (could there be a connection here with his eating habits?). His limbs were long and willowy, their motions first appearing discordant. A closer look revealed more ballet than brawn.

He had unruly, sandy-brown hair, cut short, as if by a weed-whacker, and an impish grin, as integral to his character as the food on his shirt.

He had a weak right eye. When he was lazy, agitated, or indifferent, it wandered about, not in cooperation with the left eye that locked on its subject like a mariner on Canopis. I found it disconcerting to carry on a direct conversation with Charlie while his good eye bored into me and the other danced around in search of a place to alight. The effect was even more unsettling when combined with his impish grin. But I got used to it by focusing on the good eye.

And he would do anything for kicks, short of setting himself on fire (I take it back, he did that once).

He was adventurous to the point of recklessness. If you challenged Charlie to test thin ice, he would do so. If you dared him to stomp on a cow-pie, you would lose the dare. If you bet him a nickel he wouldn't bite into a cowpie, you would be five cents lighter.

He stole matches from home regularly, and used them to experiment in making campfires, explosions, and pyrotechnical displays. He was the physicist among us who discovered that holding a lit match to the spout of a near-empty gas can is the hard way to ascertain the contents of the can.

He fancied himself a magician, claiming he could make a bullfrog disappear by the count of three. This, in fact, he accomplished by stuffing an M-80 firecracker down a bullfrog's throat and counting out three hops before it dematerialized in a fine green mist. In Charlie's world, an instantaneous change of state from solid to liquid was sufficient to constitute a disappearance.

Charlie was destined for incarceration as an adult, but we didn't see it then.

7

MY FIRST ENCOUNTER with Charlie was a year earlier, in a dense thicket of briars that hugged a dismal little creek on the outskirts of our neighborhood. I had been waltzing down the middle of the creek, skipping from rock to rock to avoid getting my shoes wet, a game that was, under the circumstances, tantamount to playing Russian Roulette.

These were the days before New Age shoes—Nikes, Pumas, and the like—when kids wore leather shoes that were clunky, rock-hard, and fashionable as combat boots. New Age shoes are impervious to any substance or condition non-nuclear. If you scrub Nikes with a wire brush, it just makes them happier; put one up to your ear like a conch shell and you will hear it calling "put me in the dishwasher." In contrast, our leather shoes were fragile as egg shells. When gotten wet—as in a romp through a mud puddle—they began a rapid deterioration. As they dried, the soles curled up like potato chips. After a few wettings and dryings, the shoes were shot. We were blue-collar folks; my dad worked in a factory and carried his lunch to work in a black lunchbox. The family car was an old Kaiser, that broke down more than it ran. The purchase of new leather shoes was a major item in the family's budget. It was important to keep them functional as long as possible. Getting them wet was a capital crime. I never once left the house in leather shoes without my mother warning, "Don't get your feet wet." I could come home at the end of the day with broken limbs and stolen merchandise and no notice would be taken if my shoes were dry.

I was concentrating so intently on skipping and keeping my shoes dry that I almost stepped on Charlie.

"Hey, watch it!" he shrieked.

He was sitting half in mud and half out, oblivious to any distinction between clean and dirty or wet and dry. He was swatting at a tiny field mouse tethered to a string tied to a branch three feet above his head. The mouse swung back and forth, as if Charlie were conducting an experiment in pendulum motion.

"Sorry," I said, stepping carefully onto dry land and out of range of the swinging mouse.

"I'm Charlie. I live across the street. This is Dwight," he said, motioning to the mouse. "He's been bad. I'm teaching him a lesson."

"What'd he do?" I said.

"He put a spell on me."

"What's a *spell*?"

"It's like a curse."

"What's a *curse*?"

"It's a ... a ... something that makes you have bad luck, or get sick or hurt ... or piss your pants in school."

"How do you know all that?" I said.

"There's this skinny old lady, lives over by Manny's Market. She's a Wiccan. Sometimes I listen outside her door at night when she has a coven, and I hear stuff."

"What's a *Wiccan*?"

"Not sure. I think it's like being Jewish, or something."

"What's a *coven*?"

"It's like a meeting."

"What do they do at the meeting?" I said.

"They wear white pajamas and hold hands and say prayers about birds and trees. And they hum a lot. Once they put a spell on Manny cuz he sells dirty books."

"What happened to him?"

"Nothing yet, I guess."

"I seen Manny yesterday," I said. "He didn't look like there's any kinda spell on'im."

"You can't always tell if somebody's got a spell on'im just by looking. He could be walking around fit as a fiddle, lookin' jes fine to you and me, and all of a sudden, drop over dead ... or just mess himself," opined Charlie, with the conviction of an expert on the paranormal.

I wasn't convinced Charlie knew what he was talking about, or that he wasn't mad as a hatter. But I found the subject quite interesting, so I ventured in a little further. "How do you know the mouse put a spell on *you*?"

"I can tell. When I grabbed him he made a spell sound, like *reek-reek-reek*. That's not all, he *looked* at me too."

"He *looked* at you?"

"Yup," he said, with such renewed conviction that I maneuvered to a frontal position where I could look at him squarely and gauge its authenticity.

"Ahhh," I inhaled quietly, stepped back a pace. This was my first experience face-to-face with Charlie's good eye and a Mexican jumping bean. It caught me by surprise.

I had more questions to ask, but I was beginning to have serious reservations about his sanity. I was trying to think of something to say that might get the conversation out of the twilight zone when he dragged me back into it.

"Ever throw scale-frogs," he said, blithely skipping on to a new subject.

"What's that?"

"You never heard of scale-frogs?"

"Nope."

"First you get some buffos—"

"What're *buffos*?" I asked.

"Bullfrogs."

"Oh."

"—then you let 'em loose on the road, say at the end of the day, when there's a lotta traffic. They get runned over and flattened, and you leave 'em there a couple days to let the sun dry 'em out. If they don't get dried out you can't scrape 'em up, they'll be too stuck to the road. So after a couple days, they're hard and dry, you scrape 'em up, and scale 'em like a shingle. They really sail when they're flat, like flying saucers."

"That's it?" I asked stupidly.

"Yeah, pretty cool, huh?"

"Yeah, cool," I said, not wanting to dampen his enthusiasm. I was now sure he was half out of his mind. But his personality was cheerful, infectious, and brimming with adventure. I thought there might be an opportunity for a unique friendship here. I was wondering how to test this hypothesis when he continued the conversation with another abrupt change of subject.

"You got a baseball bat?" he said

"Yeah, at home," I said tentatively.

"If you go get it, I'll let you have the second swing," he whispered softly, motioning to Dwight with a tilt of his head as if the mouse might hear us.

"Here we go again," I thought to myself.

Although I was not a powerful child, I was, even then, sufficiently adept at swinging a bat to be confident that if Charlie's first swing did not splatter mouse-gore all over me and my bat, my second swing would. Either way, assassination of a field mouse with my baseball bat did not seem like a good idea, so I declined Charlie's offer. I wasn't concerned about the mouse, or what my mother would say about cruelty to animals. I was concerned only about not defacing my bat. It was brand new. I hadn't even used it yet. I wanted its first contact to be with a baseball, not a mouse. My mother was indifferent to that view. I could come home with mouse gore dripping from myself and the bat and all she would say is: "Did you get your feet wet?"

This reflection was not getting us out of the twilight zone, so *I* changed the subject. "You play baseball?"

"Yeah. I love baseball," he said animatedly, both eyes fixed on me for the first time.

"C'mon then. I'll get my bat and we can find some more kids and start a game."

Apparently Charlie's attention span was short enough to forget the spell and the swinging mouse when offered the opportunity to play baseball. Especially, now that he had a new friend who owned a bat.

"Let's go," he said, jumping up and departing the creek in a flash, leaving Dwight swinging in the wind.

8

PUDGY TOOKIS WAS THE polar opposite of Charlie Miller. Pudgy was a fat florid preppy, who wasn't allowed to play with *any* of the kids in the neighborhood, especially Charlie and me. His mother had burdened him with more rules than a regiment, about which he was oddly proud, as if he enjoyed a special status in the pantheon of children and rules were his reward. He followed all his rules religiously, except the one about hanging out with Charlie and me.

Unlike Charlie, Pudgy took eating seriously. And that made him quite fat. Many of Pudgy's rules had to do with table manners and etiquette, and it seemed to me that these were an intangible restraint, without which he would just keep eating and would keep getting fatter until he exploded, like the glutton in Monty Python's *Meaning of Life*.

He was so fat, that calling him "Pudgy" was a compliment.

He was so fat that if you could wave a magic wand and make two of him from the one, they would both be fat.

His size stood in odd contrast to his wardrobe and countenance. He was always perfectly coifed, fashionably attired, and irrepressibly cheerful, all of which took the edge off his fatness.

He had slightly effeminate mannerisms, but they were mannerisms only in the simplest sense of the word, not to be confused with markers of alternative sexual persuasion.

Pudgy appreciated the qualities of friendship. He was innately honest, naturally friendly, loyal to a fault, and easy to please. A stranger might mistake his diffidence for obsequiousness, but his manner was genuine and overcame first impressions. His enjoyment of life was infectious, and preceded him. His personality clearly outshone his size. We didn't think of him as fat; we just thought of him as Pudgy.

His greatest passion was collecting butterflies. He was surprisingly agile for his size, and could chase down a prize Monarch with leaps and bounds that defied the laws of gravity. Watching Pudgy on the hunt was like watching a Road Runner cartoon.

He loved all sports. Size, attire, idiosyncrasies, and his mother's plethora of instructions did nothing to diminish his passion for a game. He was among the first to initiate, and play, any game, baseball, basketball, football, dodge ball, hockey, you name it.

His greatest thrill was bowling over an opponent in a football game. This was years before he studied Newtonian physics and fully appreciated the momentum equations, yet he knew, intuitively, that when the speed of his mass increased, the momentum of his mass increased proportionately—resulting in punishment upon an opponent increasing proportionately. Owing to this intuitive gift, Pudgy was a popular choice for fullback when sides were picked for a game.

His greatest flirtation with danger was assisting Charlie in the frog trick. He was a tag-along. He hung out with Charlie and me for the vicarious thrills, the moth to our flame. And we loved him for it.

9

CHARLIE AND I HAD FIRST met Pudgy in the schoolyard one day towards the end of the school year. The school was fairly large, and we had seen Pudgy around, but for no particular reason we had not yet made his acquaintance.

Charlie and I were with a group of kids trying to start the daily baseball game and we needed someone to play first base. We were looking around for a candidate, when we heard a ruckus coming from around the near corner of the school. I wandered over to see if there might be a first baseman there. A fat kid, smartly dressed, was surrounded by three older kids, eleven-year-olds probably, roughly dressed, who were pulling his crisply pressed shirt out of his pants and pushing him around.

The apparent leader of the older kids was a tall scruffy misfit we had never seen before. He must have just moved into the neighborhood. He was of such disheveled countenance that the word "misfit" announced him with the clarity of a ringing bell. He appeared to be of Irish extraction. He bore the characteristic face of a young Mickey Rooney, confused by the uncharacteristic voice of an old Yogi Berra. He had greasy red hair, spiked as if he had stuck his finger in a light socket, and more freckles on his face than a face should accommodate. The freckles could have softened the face had it not the feral eyes of a child raised by wolves. He had an angry smile as if his skivvies were too tight. The tableau was enhanced by erratic movements proclaiming rather than obscuring the arrival of a consummate bully. His clothes were filthy. His mind was dull.

His confederates were two equally unsavory characters we *had* seen before, hanging around the schoolyard. Both were shorter than the chief bully, in height as well as stature. They seemed attached to him more like retainers than friends. One kid was called Iggy Plickett. We didn't know the other kid's name.

Iggy Plickett's clothes were not filthy, they were loud and comical. His mother was somewhat fanciful, loopy even, and persisted in dressing him in leaf-green shirts and dark-red shorts as if he was her little gnome. His face confirmed this impression, owing to eyes—one green, one blue—spaced too close together, resembling opposite poles of a magnet seeking to collide but prevented from doing so by a wedge-shaped nose jammed between them specifically for that purpose. His mouth was equally ill-conceived. It held too-big teeth, all of them too-white. The teeth crowded the mouth, overpowering thin lips, stretching his smile into a grimace. He had the personality of a lemon, matching his expression of having eaten one.

The other kid measured three-feet, ten-inches in height, hardly tall enough to bully anyone older than four. What he lacked in height was more than compensated for by disposition akin to that of a hornet. The color palette of his clothing was gunny-sack brown, plain by comparison to Iggy. The stench of human waste clung to him perpetually like a second skin, courtesy of chronic miscommunication with toilet paper. A sharp pointed nose preceded his carriage in the way a bowsprit precedes a clipper ship. The nose was uncommonly long as if he was delivered by it, the forceps applied relentlessly until he popped free. The nose seemed more the compass of his travels than his brain. In placing his eyes and nose in a neat little group squarely on the center line of his face, the God of Symmetry had been kind. In placing a single front tooth squarely in place of the usual two, the God of Symmetry had been frivolous. He looked like a beaver.

Iggy and the beaver were fitting companions for the socket-haired bully. They didn't try to outshine him. They weren't smart enough for that. Rather, they simply mimicked his thoughts and movements as proper retainers should. As a pair, Iggy and the beaver had the combined intelligence of a woodchuck. When the bully was added to the equation, one might expect a different result, but, alas, their combined intelligence was only 1.5 woodchucks. I'd be willing to bet not one of them would get 100% on a test comprised of tying a shoelace, telling time, and adding two and two.

The fat kid was backed up against a wall of the school. He was blubbering and whimpering, clearly in distress, close on to bladder failure.

"Fat ass! Fat ass!" Socket Hair was saying, dangerously near the limits of his vocabulary, as he poked and prodded the fat kid and ruffled his perfectly combed hair.

"Leave me alone! Leave me alone!" the fat kid was saying, dangerously near the limits of his composure, as he fended off pokes and prods.

Propelled by no other interest than needing a first baseman, I started in that direction, yelling, "Hey, leave him alone!"

Socket Hair turned, took a few menacing steps in my direction, put his hands on his hips, fixed me with a withering stare, and bellowed, **"What'd you say?"**

I turned and ran back around the corner of the school to the safety of the baseball group, close on to bladder failure myself.

Pissed at myself for this display of cowardice, I sought out Charlie to discuss taking some kind of action. In recent months, for reasons unfathomable, Charlie had become my new best friend. We were inseparable.

"Charlie, Charlie," I cried. "That redheaded kid is picking on the fat kid."

"So?"

"So we gotta do something. We need someone to play first base."

"Whaddya looking at me for?" he said.

"I can't do anything alone. You see the size of that bully? You gotta help me!" I said—or rather, implored.

After this repartee, we stood there for some minutes looking at each other, me racking my brain, Charlie picking gobs of lunch from his shirt while he contemplated the situation.

"That's it!" I blurted. "That's the answer."

"Whaddya talkin' about? he said.

"Your lunch, your lunch. It's perfect."

Charlie's lunch earlier that day had been a bowl of pea soup, a main course of liver and onions, and a dessert of pumpkin pie, all of which he washed down with a glass of chocolate milk. As usual, the remains of this repast adorned the front of his person. It was a revolting spectacle that defied description and became a light in the darkness of my quandary. It was a formidable weapon.

I explained my plan to him.

Charlie had his shortcomings, but he was a loyal trooper and failing a buddy was not one of them. Moreover, he appreciated a tactical situation if it involved elements bizarre and diabolical, especially if he was to participate in it as a principal. Once recruited, he could be counted on to follow instructions to the letter, fearlessly and enthusiastically. He was up for my plan.

I gave Charlie his marching orders and watched a joyously sadistic expression envelop his face. It was beautiful. His spirit soared and he bounded off around the back of the school to an opposite corner, behind, and very near, the bullies vigorously engaged in tormenting the fat kid.

Then I slipped back around my corner of the school and headed quietly for them. Socket Hair was so singularly engaged in taunting he didn't hear me sneak up behind him.

I signaled to Charlie waiting behind the opposite corner, counted to five, and launched a body block at the back of Socket Hair's knees, the force of which caused him to fall over me, onto the ground, on his back.

My signal to Charlie had been his cue to dash towards us at full speed, which he was now doing.

I scrambled to my feet to get out of the way.

Charlie's timing was a model of the perfection a professional athlete seeks to accomplish in every performance and is fortunate to accomplish in one. At the very instant that Socket Hair landed on his back, Charlie was in the apex of a perfect swan dive, precisely over top of him.

Socket Hair looked up … a little too late.

WHOOOMMP!

Charlie landed smack on top of him, in perfect imitation of the Missionary Position.

The impact knocked the breath out of Socket Hair. As he gasped for an intake of air, I locked hands with Charlie and pulled the entire length of his lunch-besotted body over the entire length of Socket Hair, over his face, over his mouth, lips, nose, and eyes. As soon as Charlie's fly-blown shoes slid over greasy red socket-hair, he bounced up singing (to the tune of "Danny Boy"), **"Oh Greasy Boy, yer mom, yer mom is ca-a-alling—"**

The crowd cheered at Charlie's rendition of an old tune and I stood speechless.

Socket Hair lay still for several seconds, totally disoriented. Then he shook like he was going into convulsions. Then he coughed a few times. Then he made gagging sounds, caught his breath, and rolled over onto his hands and knees. He looked up at Charlie, who bowed to him deeply as if to a reigning monarch, then he looked over at me and swore to violate my sister.

Then, still on his hands and knees, he hacked up slimy gobs of silvery phlegm, half of Charlie's lunch, and all of his own.

The whole thing happened faster than Iggy and the beaver could think. Iggy just stood there, transfixed, a witless gnome statue. The beaver kid's nose had followed the action and his eyes had followed his nose, but neither organ conveyed any message to his brain—or if it did, the brain was too slow processing the information to send back a timely reply. As a consequence, neither loyal retainer provided his chief a dollop of assistance. Socket Hair would have been better served by a pair of trained seals.

Howling with laughter, we gathered up the fat kid, who said his name was Pudgy, and raced for home with him in the lead. This was our first look at Pudgy's fleet feet, and a lesson in judging a book by its cover.

A couple blocks down the street, Charlie and I stopped to catch our breath. Pudgy turned back to us and said, "That was pretty cool, thanks a lot."

"Glad we could help," I said. "You play baseball?"

"Sure, doesn't everybody?"

"I bet those bullies don't," Charlie said.

"I bet they don't even know how," I said.

Finally one of us remembered our manners. Charlie offered Pudgy his hand.

"My name's Charlie," he said. "This here's Sonny Boy," he added, gesturing at me. "Real name's Francis but he don't like it on accounta it's too girly."

"What's wrong with Frannie then? That too girly?" Pudgy asked, looking at both of us.

"Don't like that either," I said.

"So where did Sonny Boy come from?" asked Pudgy.

"Dunno."

Pudgy shrugged, indicating that was sufficient explanation. Then he scratched his head and asked Charlie, "Where'd that song come from?"

"We got some relatives who are Irish and they're always getting plastered and singing 'Danny Boy' as loud as they can. I just changed a few words, that's all."

"Well you did a pretty good job of it," Pudgy said.

"Thank you. Wanna hear some more?"

"Wasn't that good."

By now it was getting late, so we all turned to go in different directions towards our homes. Charlie still had a thought on his mind and looked over at me and asked, "How come you didn't deck that asshole for threatening your sister? He was down on his knees. You coulda cold-cocked him. And whaddya laughing at anyway?"

"I don't have a sister."

The next day we finally got around to playing baseball. Pudgy turned out to be an excellent first baseman, and a pretty good hitter too, so we were happy we had rescued him. Predictably, Charlie preferred to play catcher. He seemed to revel in the blood, sweat, and dirt that is characteristic of that position. I was the pitcher because it was my ball.

Thus we all became good friends, poised for our next adventure.

10

AS FOR ME, I was just an average white kid. I was so average I would not be noticed in a group of three. I was so average you would not be able to find me in a group photo. I was All-World in the Secret Average-White-Kid Poll.

I was also a rather charming little boy, notwithstanding the uncharacteristic lapse of judgment that is the main topic of this story. My only material flaw was disdain for the insufferable rules some mothers made stipulating who their special darlings were, and were not, allowed to play with, rules born of the arrogance of presumed superiority, rules that feed a nascent class system if left unchallenged. A mother could not be too careful in our all-white neighborhood. Little Spanky could be damaged for life if he played with the wrong kids, kids like Charlie, Pudgy and me.

I knew we were in that mix of mothers' rules somewhere, but the politics of it were too complicated to worry about that summer, so I didn't. In this regard, I championed averageness.

11

"WE GOTTA FIND A SNAKE," I said.

"Where at?" asked Pudgy.

"The Woods," offered Charlie.

"Jesus, Charlie," I cried, "are you crazy?"

Charlie never ceased to amaze me. Injury, disease, or discomfort, never seemed to enter into his decision-making process.

"The Field," said Pudgy, proclaiming the obvious.

"Thank you, Pudgy."

So off we went to the Field to find a snake.

There was a tidy public park, two blocks from my house, with a playing field used variously for baseball, football, and soccer—nobody played soccer in those days, but at least there was a place for it—and a small playground, with three swings, a slide, and a jungle-gym. The playground was crammed into a corner of the park, near the street upon which the park fronted. Behind the public park, well back from the street, ignored like a stepchild, was an untended pasture of bushes, weeds, and litter, affectionately referred to by Charlie, Pudgy, and me as the "Field."

The Field was our favorite place to play Cowboys and Indians because we were slightly taller than the weeds and bushes, therefore, we were able to see each other, and—of paramount importance—approaching enemies. No enemies had approached thus far, but that was the theory nonetheless, and it would prove to be a good one.

In other words, we were so terrified of the Woods that we instinctively sought open grassland with generous lines of sight. The Field. At age ten, we were almost as smart as the African antelope.

12

WARMING TO MY GREAT ADVENTURE, I lead my team through the neighborhood to the Field.

I was quite full of myself so I took the route that led past Janie Wagner's house. I knew Mary Lou Painter would be there with Janie, playing as usual on Janie's front porch, and I could not pass up the opportunity to impress Mary Lou with my audacious plan. I was sweet on Mary Lou.

Janie and Mary Lou were best friends. They always played at Janie's house because Janie was the most responsible of countless children in an Appalachia-size family. As such, Janie was obliged to stay by the house as the family "first responder."

Janie was uncommonly skinny, plain as mud, and wore thick glasses like the bottom of coke bottles. Her fashions were utilitarian, suitable to her job description, and sturdy enough to last through numerous levels of hand-me-downs. She was painfully alert for her age, owing to a whirlwind of unceasing activity that characterized her daily home-life. Typically, numerous siblings were engaged in an odd assortment of recreational activities, some of which flirted with criminal misdemeanor, involving, just for example, ropes, ladders, pets, paint, matches, garden tools, kitchen appliances, and homemade weapons.

The assortment of activities, practiced by any other family on the planet might be considered *common* chaos. The Wagner children, however, elevated that status to *exceptional* chaos by their affinity for—and experimentation with—*special* pets, those of various species normally incompatible with human habitation.

Here was a typical day.

A three-year-old was holding an iguana lizard upside down, trying to push it into the waistband of her pants. The lizard was of a size that required her to hold it with two hands, leaving its head free to thrash about refusing cooperation. The child's face contorted with anger and frustration, turned beet-red, and threatened to implode. She shifted her grip to the end of the beast's tail, swung it against the wall until it became more docile, then forgot about her original objective, cradled it like a baby, and sang it a song.

A four-year-old was finger painting a ferret, impervious to sights and sounds around him. He was not mute, merely focused intently on the color green, which he had discovered by accidentally mixing blue and yellow.

A six-year-old was playing mumbly-peg on the front lawn with a carving knife. Earthworms—dug up earlier with a soup spoon—were spread on the ground as moving targets, evoking a creative departure from the classic game.

A seven-year-old was looking for the carving knife, with the intention of employing it to dismember a toad on the kitchen table. He was not overly concerned with locating the sister with the knife, having secured a ball-peen hammer from the garage to serve as an alternate surgical instrument. Moreover, if he found the sister, a gentle twist of her neck would be sufficient to affect a trade of the hammer for the knife.

An eight-year-old, wearing a high-heel shoe, was attempting to drop-kick a grapefruit-size turtle into the toilet bowl in the parents' bathroom. After five or six unsuccessful attempts, she picked up the turtle, deposited it in the bowl and left the room. The smartest creature in the house at the time—besides Janie—was the turtle, who kept its head pulled into its shell, even while swimming in the bowl.

A nine-year-old, of indeterminate sex, was stalking a rabbit with a sharpened stick. He, or she, or it, was not exceptionally quick-witted, and therefore paid no attention to an infant in diapers frantically attempting to escape from a cardboard box into which a five-year-old was emptying a jar of assorted arachnids. They were the nine-year-old's arachnids and had been appropriated by the five-year-old to acquaint the infant in diapers with *God's creatures*, a notion misinterpreted from a Sunday School lesson.

A litter of kittens meowed under the back porch, whining plaintively for the return of the mother cat, a frazzled tabby named Al. Yet another child, five or six, clothed from the waist up, stood by the porch and kept Al away from the kittens with a fly swatter.

A near-featherless parrot cowered in a cage placed on the floor of the front porch. It was an African Grey, considered the best talker in the parrot family. Its only words to date had been: "Cheese-it! Cheeze-it!" It was the custom of the eight-year-old with the high-heel shoe to place the cage on the porch daily, hoping fresh air and sunshine would catalyze the growth of new feathers. The eight-year olds' attention span for dealing with the parrot was identical to that of dealing with the turtle, resulting in the bird being left out in the wind and rain on several occasions. The odds of the parrot reciting the Gettysburg Address were greater than the odds of it growing new feathers.

Along the side of the house, two family dogs, a hideous Pekingese and a three-legged Chihuahua, both the size of rats, were tethered together by a foot of rope and were fighting over a bone hauntingly similar to a human femur. It was impossible to ascertain who was responsible for the missing leg, the tethering, or the bone, as no one was in attendance at the scene.

About the only critter missing was a snake, which is why I wasn't afraid to approach the house.

It was rumored in the neighborhood that a retarded child was kept locked in an upstairs bedroom of Janie's house. We accepted this as solid fact because, whenever we passed by, we would see a shadowy face peering out through dark curtains.

I had always wondered why I never saw Janie's mother around. Years later, I learned there was no retarded child in an upstairs bedroom, only a severely unhinged mother. Janie had older brothers, identical twins, flesh-and-blood Tweedle Dee and Tweedle Dum, who had developed an unhealthy fascination with the instruments of capital punishment. They had built an electric chair for the school science fair, and somehow had tricked their mother into sitting in it. The chair was never intended to be sufficient for its historical purpose, and had, therefore, been fitted merely with token homemade electrical devices. To everyone's surprise, however, the chair proved quite sufficient for another purpose; it rearranged mother's taste buds and a host of brain cells. Sadly, mother had already commenced a slow path to madness sometime after her twelfth or thirteenth pregnancy, so a few good volts were all it took to send her completely around the bend. She had retreated voluntarily to an upstairs bedroom, and spent her remaining years there, eating oatmeal she thought was chicken, and addressing leaves on trees—in tongues.

I digress. Back to Janie. Her responsibilities left little time for grooming. Consequently, her clothes looked like they were slept in, and her hair looked like it had been on fire and was beaten out with a stick. This isn't to say she was dirty. On the contrary, she was simply a trifle frazzled. But her spirit was not affected by the mayhem around her. A stranger might think she was a little slow, when, in fact, she was just a tad shell-shocked.

She went on to become a lawyer and a Republican, if any lesson can be drawn from that.

In spite of Janie's hardships, she had an easy smile, and I liked her in a sisterly sort of way ... which, of course, was the last thing she needed.

Not surprisingly, Charlie thought Janie was the most beautiful creature on earth. The chaotic nature of Janie's home life was Charlie's version of Valhalla. Charlie thought Janie and he were a perfect fit. But Janie had seen—even through her coke-bottle glasses—the lunch encrusted on Charlie's clothes, the flies buzzing around his shoes, and the blackface he wore the day he discovered combustion. She had also been duped, once, into watching his magic trick, so any possibility of a conversation with Charlie, let alone a romance, was a non-starter. Charlie, of course, was oblivious to this.

"Hi Janie," he bellowed with enthusiasm and spittle, trying, unsuccessfully, to focus both eyes on her.

"Yuck," said Janie, under her breath, ignoring him.

"Hi," I called out, with my widest smile. I was addressing both of them to be gallant, but my greeting was intended primarily for Mary Lou.

"I'm gonna get a snake and throw it at my mother," I said proudly.

Mary Lou's face froze in a picture of complete incomprehensibility. She looked at me as if I had just spoken in Gaelic.

I didn't catch it. I was too enthralled. I was in love.

Mary Lou was the most beautiful creature on earth. She was perfect. She was literal, unlike Princess Summerfall Winterspring, a figure on a screen you could never touch. And, ooooh, was I wanting to touch.

Mary Lou's hair was shiny dark brown. It cascaded smoothly to her shoulders, and swirled in the soft wind, hypnotic and sensual.

She was wearing a new striped top that fit snugly, over light blue pedal-pushers that fit tightly. The ensemble was all of cotton, thin, and revealed every delicious fold and crease of her nubile body. Little raisin-size titties barely announced the onset of puberty.

And she stood just so, angling her body sideways, shifting her weight onto the straightened front leg, hand on her hip, pushing her butt forward, smirking imperiously. It was her signature pose … and it was just for my benefit.

"Yowzah! Yowzah!" screamed in my head.

She had a sparkle this fine summer day that got my attention like a slap in the face. This should have been a seminal event in a young boy's life. This should have been the moment when a young girl's sparkle lights up a young boy's budding sexuality.

This should have been my first boner.

But … no. Not today. Where there should have been fireworks down there, there was nothing. To paraphrase Gertrude Stein: "There was no there there." Not even a quiver.

No matter. I was only ten. There was plenty of time for the beast to mature and the crazy chase to begin.

Besides, too much other stuff was going on.

Charlie was ogling Janie, who was busy hog-tying a two-year-old.

Screams were coming from the house.

A small boy burst from an open first-floor window, landed on his head, bounced up, and ran back into the house laughing hysterically in search of another dose of whatever had propelled him through the window.

An acrid smell wafted from the kitchen, suggesting a critter had just been dispatched.

A smoldering missile flew through the air, landed at my feet, and scurried away.

Pudgy was chasing a butterfly.

Someone was watching from an upstairs window.

And I was supposed to be leading an expedition to find a snake. I had let myself get side-tracked by Mary Lou's sparkle.

I was thoroughly confused now, so I acted purely on impulse. I puffed up my chest and proudly repeated my fearless intention.

Mary Lou's face lit up like a Christmas tree in another expression of pure disbelief, which I falsely interpreted as adoration because that's what I wanted it to be.

I shivered with excitement and turned to go.

As I continued on up the street, a jumble of emotions gave way to a realization that I had just crossed a threshold of sorts. In the presence of my mates, and *in front of girls*, I had shot off my big mouth about this great gag I was going to play on my mother. Now I had to do it. There was no turning back.

I felt the onset of panic. Had I not been so self-absorbed, I might have looked back for another shot of Mary Lou's butt. And had I done so, I might have seen Janie and Mary Lou huddling together, chuckling. I might even have heard Janie say to Mary Lou, "Boys are really dumb." And Mary Lou reply, "What a moron."

Apparently, Mary Lou and I were on quite different wavelengths. But since I didn't know that, I continued merrily on my lovesick way.

Finally we reached the field. It was time for things to get real. The day was warm and clear. No clouds marred the sky. No one else was about to disturb the tranquil setting. It was a perfect snake day? It was time to do the deed. It was time to actually find a snake, as I said I would.

I began to rummage about in the grass absently—stalling is more like it. As the cold truth of this venture set in, I rehearsed some graceful excuses to back out: "No snakes today boys, sorry," or, "It's getting late guys, time to go home."

I had really done it this time. I began to panic.

In typical testosterone-fueled fashion, I had enlisted Charlie and Pudgy purely for self-aggrandizement, without fully contemplating the consequences. I had made myself the alpha male and now I had to perform.

I had to *capture* and *hold* a snake, hence the panic.

13

THE PROBLEM OF HOW to *capture* a snake is simple: pin its head down with a forked stick.

The problem of how to *hold* a snake is an entirely different matter because it involves actually touching the thing: grip it behind the head with thumb and forefinger and pick it up.

Easy to say, but this is the hard part, because precisely at the point of grabbing it, the insidious beast will wrap its slimy body around your arm and will writhe and squirm and constrict against your bare flesh in frantic electric spasms. This will cause your heart to skip a beat, and you might shit your pants.

The sole objective of a snake at this point, any snake, is to squeeze you, or bite you, or scare you, or all of those, until you are sufficiently incapacitated so it can swallow you whole, head first. That is all a snake cares about—head-first swallowing. That's its job. It has no conscience. It is completely indifferent to Science, Art and Politics. It doesn't care if you are rich or poor, short or tall, young or old. It doesn't care if you are constipated or incontinent. It doesn't care if you are Caucasian, Eurasian, Pygmy, or Protestant. It doesn't care if you are homosexual, heterosexual, or transsexual. It doesn't care if you are naked or wearing Nikes and a backpack. It only cares about unhinging its jaws and sliding its lips over your head and gulping and gulping until you are entirely inside its skin and its enzymes are reducing you to mush and absorbing you into its system.

If a snake gets you by the head, there is no escape. You cannot pull it off. You are a goner. It will stretch and gulp and continue gulping until it gets all of you. You can dash about waving your arms and screaming that there is a snake on your head but it won't do any good. Eventually it will work its way down over your eyes and nose and mouth so you can't scream anymore, and then over your shoulders and down over your arms so you can't flail about anymore. Finally, it will work its way down over your knees and squeeze your legs together and you will fall down and it will continue gulping no matter how big your shoes are until no part of you is showing and there is nothing left except a big fat happy snake lying on the ground digesting a lump in its belly.

This can happen because the smallest snake can swallow the largest head. A tiny Green Mamba can swallow Knute Gingrich.

Knowing this, you realize that once you have grabbed hold of a snake you cannot just let go, because if you do it will jump up onto your head and then you are finished. And as you hang on to the snake you have so unwisely grabbed hold of, trying to figure a way out of your predicament, the sonofabitch will squirm faster and squeeze harder. Droplets of sweat will form on your brow. Your heart will jerk like a jackhammer and your bladder will fail and you will enter stage one of a nervous breakdown.

That, my friend, is *holding a snake.*

When my Time on Earth is up, and I am received at the Gates of Paradise and offered the choice of holding a snake or of nailing my foot to the floor and running around it in circles for all eternity, I shall choose the latter.

14

EVENTUALLY I REALIZED that I could dither no longer. Time to perform. I found a forked stick, about five feet long, that would keep a viper at a comfortable distance until I could work my way down the stick to its head.

Then I began to thrash about in the weeds for the snake. I thrashed tentatively, while Charlie and Pudgy thrashed with the genuine enthusiasm of non-combatants. Silently, I beseeched the Gods to rid the Field of serpents, to grant me a face-saving excuse to call it a day.

And apparently the Gods heard me. After an hour or so of thrashing, we had encountered no snake. By then, the sun had set and it was starting to get dark. This was the time of day when all little boys *must*, on pain of a whipping, head for home. This I did, having no choice in the matter.

Whew! I felt like I had escaped a bullet.

On the way home, we passed Janie's house. Mary Lou was still there, chatting on the front porch with Janie. There was no mayhem about, and the place was eerily quiet. A beat-up Studebaker stood in the driveway, indicating that either the father home from work or the social worker on a routine visit was responsible for the semblance of normalcy.

The only visible activity was provided by a six-year-old, the sister with initial possession of the carving knife. Apparently she had, since, traded it without duress to the seven-year-old for the ball-peen hammer. She was now engaged in tapping the hammer on a walnut placed on the concrete sidewalk in front of the porch. The child's face was scrunched in anger and intensity, the tapping a gentle prelude to an imminent overhand blow, sure to render the nut meat inedible—if indeed edibility was ever the objective.

Mary Lou called out, "Where's the snake, hotshot?"
"Couldn't find one," I said sheepishly.
"Bet you didn't try very hard," she said.
"I did, I did," I said, not believing the lie.
"Right," she said, nailing me with embarrassment.

15

I WAS HAVING SECOND THOUGHTS about this snake gag. I was sorely in need of a diversion to collect my thoughts and figure a way out … or in, if that was my destiny. I recalled a special attribute of Pudgy and wondered how it might serve my purposes.

Pudgy was Snackman, owing to an attribute uncommonly rare for a ten-year-old kid in a family of moderate means in a lily-white neighborhood in New England in the middle of the twentieth century: he could find a snack anywhere. A snack *outside* the home, that is. A snack in addition to the volumes of food he consumed *inside* the home. He could *find* a snack with a skill superior to that of a driver ant. He could *make* a snack, *wheedle* a snack, *conjure up* a snack, or *squeeze* a snack out of a turnip. He could *cause* a snack to find him.

Had the government been aware of this attribute, Pudgy would have been secreted away in the night to the bowels of the most secret chambers and subjected to endless hours of medical experiment to learn his secret—in the interests of national security of course.

Homemade baked goods, those from the kitchens of the neighborhood, were his specialty. He could divine a pie being baked before its scents wafted on the air. Pastries, too. Cookies were his favorite. He could anticipate the baking of cookies as if the mixing of the dough sent photons of early-warning energy only to him. He could materialize on a neighbor's doorstep, at the precise moment in time a batch of newly baked cookies had cooled, with an eminently plausible reason for being there unrelated to the baking of the cookies, bearing an expression of innocence that suggested he was about to expire from malnutrition and only a cookie could save him. No mother could resist this ruse.

And there were the growing snacks, the farm crops, for which the summer and fall of 1952 Connecticut belonged to Pudgy. There were several farms all around our neighborhood, bristling with goodies, calling Pudgy by name as they ripened. His aptitude for determining ripeness exceeded that of the eldest farmer. A sixth sense. Internal radar told him where and when to find any edible crop: apples, pears, peaches, plums, cherries, watermelon, cantaloupe, carrots, peppers, tomatoes, and potatoes, to name a few.

When Pudgy got that special hunger pang—the one he claimed plagued him like an itch he can't scratch—he summoned Charlie and me for companionship. With the team formed, he would charge off in a frenzy, frothing at the mouth, eyes glazed over. His singular anticipation was ardent, pre-sexual, and beautiful to behold.

We loved to follow Pudgy when his radar was on. It was up to us to keep up with him. And we did. Charlie and I were always up for a snack anyway. You'd think we weren't fed at home. The irony was in the meager quantities Charlie and I consumed: sliver of an apple, bite of a pepper, a few blackberries. Paltry morsels were quite enough for the two of us. It didn't take much. The smallest token can satisfy the appetite of a normal ten-year-old (Pudgy, of course, not being normal in this context). Quantities do not become aberrational until the teenage years. But *quantity* was never the issue. An apple stolen satisfies so much more than an apple given.

Pudgy had it figured out. He said we were not petty thieves; we would not raid private gardens. We would only hit the large fields of the local farmers. He said we shouldn't view it as stealing, on the theory that our impact on hundreds of acres of crops was insignificant, inconsequential. Charlie and I could buy that. So we went along with Pudgy, comfortable with his homespun *no-big-deal* theory of law. Besides, we couldn't go rummaging around in small private gardens anyway, we were too big for that, too *detectable*. We'd be caught in heartbeat. So why try?

We were practical when it came to snack-finding. As a consequence, most of the farmers knew us, and didn't care if we snatched a tomato or two, as long as we didn't trample the plants. The element of constructive consent was an additional comfort to our rather flexible conscience.

There were other snacks Pudgy could find. These were the fruits that grew wild and were available for the taking if one knew where to look, which Pudgy did. Blackberries, raspberries, black raspberries, and elderberries grew plentifully in the cow pasture just up the hill.

The cow pasture was sprinkled with apple trees that never bore red apples, and was lined at its lowest point with the briars and bushes that bore the several varieties of berries. I loved berries; they were my favorite. Were it not for the briars, I would have spent more time in the bushes and surely would have gorged myself on berries and been in trouble at the supper table for not finishing my meal. Briars were good for something.

I had been forbidden to play in the cow pasture, but I did anyway. Stealth and agility were required in order to keep this from my mother. There were, in addition to several lazy cows in the pasture, three baby bulls. There was no papa bull, and although I was puzzled by this oddity, I preferred ignorance to an inquiry that would certainly reveal my disobedience. A favorite pastime was throwing green apples at the baby bulls, chasing them around the pasture. Stealth was required to sneak up on the bulls, and agility was required to avoid stepping in cow-pies while chasing them.

Chasing the bulls was another activity tantamount to playing Russian Roulette. The lathering of cow dung upon leather shoes was the first cousin of getting them wet. No matter the relationship, the reward would be the same.

And there were snacks that could only be purchased at a market, such as candy, cookies, and soda pop. Occasionally, one of us could squeeze a nickel or two out of a parent. More often than not, we had to earn money or find it. Pudgy's favorite solution was a combination of the two: find empty soda bottles thrown by the wayside, and redeem them at a market for cash. Twelve-ounce bottles were worth two cents. Quart bottles were the big prize, worth a nickel. When you saw a quart bottle, you saw a candy bar, like a mirage in the desert.

Soda bottles could be redeemed at most markets, provided they were not cracked or broken. Any condition short of cracked or broken was accepted, sometimes grudgingly, as in the time Charlie found a coke bottle covered in gunk. "Check this out," he said to Pudgy and me one day, the good eye fixed on us, the other on the bottle. "Looks like it just been pulled from a horse's ass. Let's see if the guy'll take it."

Pudgy and I followed behind, trying to look like we weren't involved. Flies buzzed around Charlie and the bottle as he tendered it to the grocer. The man was very annoyed, but he accepted the bottle gracefully, all the while delivering a stern lecture on the subject of personal hygiene.

The episode taught us that, in dealing with an ornery grocer, the prudent course was to smile innocently rather than blubber a lame excuse. It should have taught us to wash off the bottles. At ten, we got away with what we could. Has anything changed?

Pudgy was the bottle-finding champion though. The Snackman, in every respect. He could find discarded bottles with a special radar, akin to his cookie-finding radar, as if bottles emanated the aroma of the treat he would buy with the proceeds of their redemption. Sounds biblical. To Pudgy it was.

A special spot by the railroad tracks seemed to store bottles there, magically, for safe keeping, just for Pudgy. Charlie and I knew about the special spot, but we never tried to beat Pudgy to it. One did not tamper with that kind of magic. Besides, there was no need. Pudgy shared everything he had with us, whether found, wheedled, pilfered, or purchased. There was no reason to compete with him. We were happy just to tag along and encourage the honing of his snack-finding attributes.

Pudgy's fortune was our fortune, a form of childhood socialism.

16

ONE DAY WHILE we were out foraging for snacks, Farmer Quigley rumbled up in his pick-up truck and invited us to have *lunch*—on his property—with his vegetables. This was very good news from my point of view, whatever it really meant, as it represented another event to divert attention from the subject of my snake gag.

"What's for lunch?" Pudgy asked Farmer Quigley.

"Potatoes."

"What else?" said Pudgy.

"Just potatoes."

"That's it?"

"Yup."

"That doesn't sound so good," said Pudgy, scratching his head. He was our negotiator when it came to snack issues.

Farmer Quigley smiled, swatted at a fly, and said, "Baked potatoes, actually. Look over there."

He pointed to a wisp of smoke coming from the far corner of the potato patch he had combed with his tractor a few days before. The tractor had pulled a harvester that dug potatoes out of the ground and dumped them into a bin, leaving uprooted potato plants in the wake. Earlier today, Farmer Quigley had combed up the potato plants, now wilted and dry, put them in a pile at the far corner of the field, and set them on fire, as was the custom of disposal. The wisp of smoke was coming from the fire.

"The harvester never gets all them potatoes," he said. "There are always a few left over in the furrows. What you do is, poke around and find some, throw 'em in the fire and leave 'em there until the fire burns down to hot coals, then pull 'em out with a stick, and you got baked potatoes."

So we did.

Pudgy was thrilled to learn a new snack-finding skill; Charlie was doubly thrilled to find fire and food combined into a single event; and I was in hog-heaven because I loved baked potatoes.

At some point in our enjoyment of the new-found cuisine, Farmer Quigley rumbled up in his pickup truck to see how we were doing. With an amusing smile brightening his weathered face, he offered us a drink from a half-gallon, glass jug he carried around in the truck behind the seat. The stuff in the jug was a little cloudy due to fermentation, but we didn't know what fermentation was so it didn't register any concern.

"What is that?" Pudgy asked.

"Apple Cider."

"It don't look like Apple Cider. It's all cloudy."

"It's just shook up from bouncin' around in the truck."

"Okay," said Pudgy, taking a healthy swig.

Charlie and I watched as he handed the jug back to Farmer Quigley, grimaced, gagged, regurgitated some of it, and crossed his eyes, as the remainder shot down his throat.

Farmer Quigley chuckled.

Charlie stepped over, grabbed the jug from Farmer Quigley and took a long deep hit. Most of it went into his mouth. Some of it went down the front of his shirt where it belonged. He smiled, apparently unaffected. Fermentation seemed to agree with him as if there was a genetic association. Then he took another big hit and handed the jug to me. We both stood motionless for a few seconds, some intuition telling us to wait for the effect. Then one eye glazed over while the other one jumped around avoiding the glazing as if it were a pesky mosquito. He smiled, stumbled backwards a few steps, smiled again absently, turned around, and pitched face-first onto the ground where he had been seated earlier dissecting a potato. His face plowed into soft dirt two inches from the potato, which is the first thing he saw as he opened his eyes. "Cool!" he said, and laughed hysterically. Then he sat up unfazed and resumed work on the potato without even brushing the dirt from his face.

I stood dumbly, enjoying the Charlie Show and assessing my turn with the cider. I looked at the cloudy concoction in the jug, at the slobber Charlie had left on the rim of the jug, at Pudgy making gagging gestures, and handed the jug back to Farmer Quigley, who shook his head and laughed.

The jug incident did not, however, diminish my enjoyment of the baked potatoes. Without water or cider they were a little dry, but I gorged on them nonetheless until I could gorge no more. That night I couldn't eat a bite of my supper and was compelled to explain why. The day ended inauspiciously, with a token spanking and early retirement.

17

PUDGY WAS RESTIVE. "I wanna kill him," he said.

"Whaddya talking about," I said. "Kill who?"

"The red-headed bully kid."

"He's too big," I said. "Besides, you can't just kill someone. It's against the law."

Pudgy had spent a few days reflecting on his treatment at the hands of Socket Hair, and now he was seething with hatred. A small gaggle of girls, including Janie and Mary Lou, had witnessed the event, adding public embarrassment to his personal humiliation. Pudgy had been rescued, but had not played any role in it. He wanted to redeem himself with his own revenge. He had been trying to figure that out when he had blurted carelessly, "I wanna kill him."

The timing of Pudgy's predicament suited my purpose perfectly. I had over-sold the snake gag and, in so doing, had even frightened myself. I needed diversions to stretch out the time until everyone forgot about it.

"Yeah, yeah, I know I can't kill him. The question is, what *can* I do?" said Pudgy.

Perfect, I thought, now I've got something to work on.

"Let's find Charlie and have a war conference," I said.

"Good idea," said Pudgy, apparently sharing my belief that Charlie's participation in staging an act of revenge would not only be advisable, it would be indispensable.

Finding Charlie, of course, was easier said than done.

He wasn't at home.

He wasn't in the schoolyard.

He wasn't at the ball field.

Finally, we saw a wisp of smoke coming from the thicket of briars down at the creek, and we knew that would be him.

We ran over.

Charlie was sitting there, half in and half out of the mud as usual, tending a small fire he had made with newspaper and leaves. Dwight still hung from a branch behind him, shriveled, black, and quite dead. A rough smell lingered in the air, wrinkled my nose, but did not seem to bother Charlie. He was busy roasting tadpoles on a sharp stick as if they were marshmallows. He looked up.

"If you do it just right, they pop," he said.

Three blackened charcoals by his side suggested that he hadn't got it *just right* yet. His enthusiasm was not dampened by failure as he methodically rotated the tadpole, aiming for the right feel.

"Charlie, Charlie," I said, affecting a superior tone. "They ain't gonna pop the way yer doin' it."

"Whaddya mean?"

"You're puncturing 'em with the stick. They can't blow up cuz you already put a hole in 'em. If they can't blow up, they can't pop," I said pompously. Mr. Science.

He thought about it for a minute, then smiled and said, "Hunh, maybe you got something there."

Meanwhile, Pudgy was getting impatient seeing the subject of his visit getting lost in a discussion about blowing up tadpoles. He could see that the next order of business would be consideration of an instrument to replace the sharp stick and he'd never get his problem solved, so he chimed in with, "Forget that, please! I need some help here. I wanna get revenge on that frizzy-haired kid for pushing me around the other day."

"We already did that," said Charlie, looking wistfully at the stick with a sizzling tadpole stuck to it.

I figured I better help Pudgy. With an air of authority, I said, "Charlie, c'mon, he's right. Forget that! Pudgy needs to get his own revenge. He needs to do something to that bully. Something he won't forget. Something *dirty*."

The last word was a magic one to Charlie. A deep tone vibrated in his psyche like an alurum bell lightly stuck. He sat up, flipped the stick and tadpole away, and stared straight ahead for a full minute. Both eyes focused on an object in the creek. Perhaps thoughts were forming inside his head. Perhaps he was hearing music. Something was happening.

In any event, we had his attention. So we waited silently.

Then he jumped up, stomped on the fire, turned to leave, changed his mind, sat down again, looked up at Pudgy and me standing there, and said, "Okay you guys, where ya goin'? Sit down and let's figure this out."

So we sat.

And thought.

Nobody moved.

After a few minutes, Charlie said, "Pudgy can't do anything alone, that kid's too big. We gotta help him (*no shit, Charlie, that's why we're here*, I thought but didn't say it). And one weeny little trick for revenge ain't gonna be enough to get him off Pudgy's back. He needs a lesson that messing with Pudgy is unhealthy."

Pudgy and I sat quietly, appearing to contemplate this pronouncement, but really waiting for the next one.

After another minute, Charlie continued. "I got it, I got it. Not one lesson, he needs two lessons. One won't be enough. That kid's too nasty. He'll just come back after Pudgy again. Pudgy hasta zing him twice to be sure he gets the message."

Pudgy and I looked at each other and nodded agreement. Charlie had, inside of four minutes, articulated a brilliant concept.

After further discussion, we decided to reconnoiter the neighborhood for useful objects, situations, and circumstances with which to develop our plan of attack.

Later in the week, I learned that the skinny old Wiccan lady Charlie had referred to at our first meeting was Socket Hair's mother. Apparently her religious persuasion was a not-so-secret secret in the neighborhood. I heard my parents discussing it one night in hushed tones so I wouldn't hear them. I couldn't make out their entire conversation, but I caught a few snippets, "... Wicca ... neopagan ... Horned-God ... meet in covens ... Great Mother Goddess ... Sylphs ... Gnomes...." This did little to illuminate me on the nature of the obscure religion, but it was sufficient to convince me that the mother was a witch. The next day, I related this intelligence to Charlie and Pudgy.

After considerable discussion, we decided that we didn't care if Socket Hair's mother was a witch or a warlock; we only cared if we could put the knowledge to some advantage. We were liberal little kids. Practical to a fault.

Charlie observed that if Socket Hair was raised by a witch-mother, who mixed potions and cast spells, then he probably believed in—or, at the very least, would recognize—visits from the Beyond. Here was a potential weapon for Pudgy's arsenal.

Two weeks later, after hours of research and planning, we reached some conclusions. We decided that the theme of Lesson #1 would be *Fear and Destruction*, and the theme of Lesson #2 would be *Pain*. We also decided the instruments and dates of execution.

18

ON THE NIGHT BEFORE Lesson #1, after everyone was asleep, Pudgy sneaked out of his house, crept through the neighborhood to Socket Hair's house, tapped on his bedroom window, and shined a flashlight into the room until he woke up. From our clandestine reconnoiter of the neighborhood we had learned that Socket Hair's bedroom was on the first floor of the house, at the back corner. Pudgy would be able to stand between the house and some bushes, unseen from the street, and just barely reach the window with the flashlight.

Pudgy continued flashing light around the room until Socket Hair came to the window to see what was going on. At that instant, Pudgy shined the flashlight on a cardboard sign he held up in his other hand, upon which was scrawled, "Pudgy is Fear." He watched carefully as Socket Hair struggled to comprehend what he was seeing. When Pudgy sensed that comprehension had registered, he flipped the sign around to display on its other side, "and Destruction." When he was satisfied that this half of the message registered as well, he cut and ran.

The next day, we hid in the bushes and watched Socket Hair in his yard working on his pride and joy: a homemade buggy he hoped to enter in the local Soap Box Derby. He had affixed an old steamer trunk to a wood frame, to which was attached a fixed rear axle with large baby carriage wheels and a movable front axle with small baby carriage wheels. The steamer trunk was the body of the vehicle, as if he were making a touring coach rather than a racing car. He had cut a small rectangle in the front side of the trunk for vision, a windshield of sorts, without glass. There were no such holes for vision on the sides or rear. A rope for steering was attached to the right and left sides of the front axle and looped into the trunk through holes cut in the front corners of it. There was no braking mechanism. And it was big enough for a single passenger, if one were so foolish. It was a perfect monstrosity, a death trap. And Socket Hair had made it just for us.

A few days later, we hid behind a house and watched a typical voyage of the buggy. It took place on a street with a steep downhill incline, where propulsion due to gravity led to a four-way intersection marked with two stop signs, one facing up the incline, one opposite, allowing cross-traffic to zip through the intersection unchecked. The downhill street continued through the intersection, becoming a long level run-out. Safe passage through the intersection required trusty lookouts to signal the absence of oncoming traffic. The trusty lookouts were also required to do double-duty as external brakemen, owing to the buggy's lack of a braking mechanism. Iggy and the other kid were the lookouts and the brakemen. This appeared to be the only useful purpose they served.

I thought it took some cojones to enclose oneself in a steamer trunk with no brakes and careen down a hill in it, relying on two half-wits for life or death decisions. I also thought it took a leave of one's senses.

What we needed next was a *grand* leave of one's senses. We needed that one day when Socket Hair's friends were not around and he was stupid enough to roll alone. Odds were good we'd get one.

Sure enough, several days later, Charlie came running. "He's going alone, he's going alone, c'mon, c'mon," he cried. His face beamed gold with excitement and his eyes worked in harmony.

We knew what he meant.

We gathered up the dirty blanket Charlie brought from home, ran over to the hill, and watched from behind a house.

Socket Hair had pushed his racer from his house to the top the hill and was standing proudly by it like an Indy 500 driver. Then he puffed up his chest and looked around for an audience (oh this was too much, I thought). Finding none, he put one leg inside the steamer trunk, checked that the intersection below was clear, put the rest of himself in the trunk, let the lid down, and started to roll.

Before the buggy could pick up any momentum, we ran out from behind the house and stopped it. Pudgy threw the dirty blanket over the front of the trunk, putting its interior in total darkness, and clamped his bulk down on the lid.

Socket Hair began yelling and kicking inside the box. We had to act fast before he kicked his way out, or somebody heard him, or both.

We had stopped the buggy while it was still at the top of the hill because we had a different direction—and a different incline—in mind for it.

One block over was Scripps Pond, a small stagnant oasis of murky water and lily pads at the bottom of a natural depression one might easily mistake for an abandoned quarry. The walls of the depression, hillsides really, crisscrossed with trails and footpaths—shortcuts into town—were untended and overgrown. Weeds, bushes, and mature trees grew all the way down to the water line. In winter, older kids played hockey on the ice, while we sledded down the snowy hillsides onto it. There was a favorite spot on the top of the hillsides towards which we now maneuvered the buggy, as fast as our little legs would go.

Huffing and puffing, we finally reached the spot. We paused momentarily to regard the steepness of the hillsides and the filthiness of the water below. This was our favorite spot—for launching sleds. Gravity provided our steel-bladed sleds with instant acceleration, and was sure to do the same to the buggy which, without further ado, we now let go.

The buggy lurched forward, accelerated properly, careened downhill for several yards, swiped a tree, bounced off a rock, and jumped a foot in the air. Muffled screams from inside the box wafted in the air. The front of the buggy arced downward and the front wheels dug into the ground, their motion arrested. The steamer trunk separated

from the frame, continued its downhill journey, flipped over, and burst open, ejecting Socket Hair. He tumbled over a few times and came to rest at the bottom of the slope, half in the mud and half out. He was terrified but unhurt. The buggy was in shambles.
Fear and Destruction.
So far, so good.

We were accused of committing this atrocity. But it had been a slow time of day, nobody was around, and nobody had seen a thing. With no witnesses, nothing could be proved. We had used hand signals exclusively, so there was no chance of voice recognition. When the buggy flipped over and we saw that Socket Hair was still alive, we had vanished like smoke in a windstorm.

Socket Hair could claim that Pudgy had visited him in the night with an implied threat, but nobody would believe that, even if he could articulate it.

So he had limped home and complained to his mother, but got no sympathy whatsoever from her. The few minor bruises he showed her were nothing new. He was always coming home ragged and torn. His mother was not about to make a fuss based on flimsy evidence—no evidence really. Moreover, Wicca was considered such an off-beat religion that she preferred to keep a low profile in the neighborhood. And even more to our favor, she was glad to see the end of the stupid buggy. She never liked it in the first place.

But Socket Hair knew. That was our objective. So you could say: a good time was had by all.

19

A WEEK LATER, we started work on Lesson #2.

We went to Manny's Market and got a medium-size cardboard box. Charlie scrawled "A SPeLL on YOU" on two sides of it in large black letters. On the other two sides of the box he drew a crude pentacle, the Wicca symbol that we found in a book at the library: a circle with a five-pointed star inside, the points of the star connected to the circle's circumference.

Inside the box Charlie placed a piece of wood with "Pudgy is Pain" carved into it, the grooves blackened with the ashes of roasted tadpoles.

When no one was looking, Charlie placed the cardboard box, with its contents, next to Socket Hair's bicycle at school. We should have been concerned about physical evidence, but we were only ten, remember?

20

OUR NEIGHBORHOOD WAS a pleasant collection of one-story clapboard houses built on small lots in a pre-World War II subdivision. *Houses* may be an exaggeration. They were small, two-bedroom, one-bath, cottages really, with full basements used mostly as a storage room for garden tools and a holding pen for obstreperous children. Houses were heated by coal-fired furnaces, stoked like an old steam locomotive with shovelfuls of anthracite coal. A coal bin occupied one corner of the basement next to the stairs. If there was anything worse than getting your feet wet, it was playing in the coal bin. Most kids only did this once.

The houses were built with sharp peaked roofs to discourage the accumulation of snow. The roofs were topped with asphalt shingles, an economic building material largely effective to repel the elements. Stairs led from an inside hallway to the unfinished area beneath the roof, the attic, where family albums, heirlooms, and abandoned athletic equipment were stored. Monsters lurked in these attics at one time; but they had usually fled by age seven or eight.

Originally there were no garages or other frills, however, some families had added porches, garages, dormers, and the like, depending on the size of their lot and their pocketbook. We could not afford these improvements so our house remained exactly as originally built. The family car, the old Kaiser, sat in the driveway, in sun, sleet, rain, or snow. Pudgy's house had a garage, otherwise his house and Charlie's looked exactly like mine, except for the color.

Streets were narrow, two-lane, configured in rectangular patterns, forming small blocks and an occasional cul-de-sac. Sidewalks and curbs fronted every house. Sidewalks were good for roller-skating, and curbs were good for bike-jumping.

The neighborhood was tidy, blue-collar white, socially and racially homogenous. Most everyone was on a first-name basis with their neighbors next door, their neighbors across the street, and everybody else within a mile radius.

These were the days when family dogs ran free, and you could borrow a cup of sugar from your neighbor. Mothers wore housedresses, and generally weren't very pretty. Milk in glass bottles was delivered to your back door by a milkman in a white uniform who took the empties set out and replaced them with full ones he knew from memory the family wanted. There was a breadman too, but we got our bread at the A&P because my dad used that as an excuse to go there so he could buy cheap beer at the liquor store next door.

As the neighborhood matured, fences announcing property lines emerged gradually like mold. Most fences were less than four feet high, made with flimsy chicken wire. A few were higher, and some were made with wood slats. The fences were effective to retain family pets, but were merely minor irritants to ten-year-old boys. There wasn't a fence in the neighborhood we couldn't scale in a nanosecond, no matter how high it was. The higher the fence, the longer the drop on the other side. Big deal.

One wood fence in particular, between Old Man Kramers' house and Charlie's, had been installed by Old Man Kramer to discourage us from using his backyard as a short cut. Old Man Kramer had no appreciation for the premise that the shortest distance between two points is a straight line. Charlie, Pudgy, and I had no appreciation for frustrations of that premise. To deprive a kid of a shortcut was a tyranny.

Old Man Kramer's lot was rectangular in shape, long and narrow, front to rear. His house was positioned near the front of the lot, leaving a long backyard in which he grew flowers and vegetables in a small well-tended garden. Across the rear of the lot, where the backyard ended abruptly and the Woods began, there was no fence. None was needed. The Woods—into which we would surely not venture and therefore surely not emerge—were as much a fence as a stone wall.

Old Man Kramer's fence extended straight as an arrow, from the sidewalk at the front of his lot, to the Woods at the rear of his lot. A dense overgrown forsythia bush, planted by Old Man Kramer years ago, sat next to the fence six feet in from the Woods. The bush obscured the six foot section of the fence between it and the Woods such that Old Man Kramer could not see that part of the fence from his house. In that section of fence we had made a hole by prying two slats off the upper and lower cross-beams. The height of the upper cross-beam was such that we could zip through the hole on a dead run without ducking. Anyone taller could not.

Late one afternoon, shortly after Lesson #1, we noticed Socket Hair meandering down the street towards Old Man Kramer's house. We suspected he was up to no good, so we watched surreptitiously from behind Charlie's house. Assuming no one was watching, Socket Hair slipped behind Old Man Kramer's house, found our hole in the fence, and examined it closely. In a rare display of computation, he figured out that the top of his head was a few inches higher than the bottom of the upper cross-beam. He looked around to double-check that no one was watching, and, satisfied, took three quick trial-runs through the hole, perfecting a ducking maneuver. Convinced he had mastered the timing of it, he disappeared as quickly as he had arrived.

Clearly, Socket Hair had some devious plan in mind for us. He wouldn't be skulking around in the two backyards if he wanted to shake our hands and give us a big hug. Unwittingly, however, he had given us the final piece of our plan for him.

21

THE DAY AFTER PLACING the cardboard box next to Socket Hair's bicycle, Pudgy threw an egg at him from behind a fence at the baseball field, and called out a quaint salutation, **"Hey dickhead!"**

Socket Hair responded immediately with another. **"You sonofabitch,"** he bellowed, and took off after Pudgy.

Pudgy was swift enough to stay ahead of Socket Hair for the block and a half to Old Man Kramer's place. But Socket Hair was bigger and faster, and slowly began to close the gap. This was anticipated, and was part of the plan.

Pudgy dashed around the corner of Old Man Kramer's house, fled behind the vegetable garden, and made for the hole in the fence. Socket Hair was so close on Pudgy's tail, he could almost touch him. Pudgy zipped through the hole. Socket Hair sought to follow, his speed at its fastest, his rage at its blindest, confident that his imminent execution of the ducking maneuver would put Pudgy in his grasp.

Charlie and I were in Charlie's yard, behind the fence, on either side of the hole, holding a short length of a two-by-four behind the upper cross-beam. We were positioned so that the two-by-four and the two of us could not be seen by anyone approaching from Old Man Kramer's yard. The hole in the fence was oh so inviting.

Socket Hair hit the hole on a dead run, performed the ducking maneuver perfectly, just as Charlie and I lowered the hidden two-by-four.

CLUNK!

Forehead-in-Motion to Wood-at-Rest.

Wood wins.

Socket Hair never knew what hit him. He fell back into Old Man Kramer's yard, dazed and confused.

Before he had a chance to figure things out, we ran into Charlie's house, taking the two-by-four with us, and scurried down the stairs into the basement. We pulled two chairs over to a small window facing the backyard and all three us crowded onto the chairs to see what we could see.

Through the hole in the fence we saw Socket Hair sprawled on his back, struggling to clear his head and gather his thoughts. Eventually, he fumbled to his feet and stood. A puzzled look wrinkled his brow as he wondered if he had misjudged the ducking maneuver or if he had been outwitted again. He could come to no immediate conclusion, which was nothing new and therefore didn't overly concern him. He was used to operating with a certain level of confusion and uncertainty.

He took a few tentative steps and staggered out of Old Man Kramer's yard, reeling as if he just got off a fast-moving merry-go-round.

Eventually he would figure it out.

But for now, *Pain* was upon him.

The stars were aligned.

22

I BRIGHTENED WHEN SUMMER FADED and baseball season moved over to make room for football season. I brightened, not because baseball season was waning, but because football season gave me an opportunity to involve my peers in a new endeavor, hopefully erasing from their memory forever my false braggadocio and reluctance to perform the snake trick.

Football was as much loved as baseball amongst the kids in our parts, so the transition from one to the other at the end of summer was always seamless. It made sense. The cooler weather required a transition from tee shirts and shorts to sweatshirts and dungarees. The latter constituted the proper uniform for football anyway.

There was only one kind of football: tackle. If you were a boy, you played tackle football. That was it. End of story. Touch football was not a part of your vocabulary, except in the very rare instance when you played with girls. And then you played touch only if they insisted. Boys prefer tackle, for more reasons than one.

There was a core group of us kids in the neighborhood that played some version of a football game almost every day. The game, fundamentally, was football; the version differed only in the number of kids playing. There was, however, a minimum number required to constitute a game; that was four, two on a side. On offense, one to hike and then block or go out for a pass, and the other to pass or run; on defense, two to impede the offense until they got their turn at it. Any number of players *more* than four gave rise to a serious game; any number *less* than four was a dilemma.

There were *little* games and *big* games, generally speaking.

A little game was four or five or six kids total, and could be played on a plot of frazzled grass inside a traffic circle across from my house. The playing area was the size of a tennis court; the goal lines were where the grass met the street. A touchdown could only be scored by running off the traffic circle into the street; so we learned to watch out for cars at a very early age. There was no such thing as an end zone, nor any need for one.

A big game could be seven or eight kids, or thirty, depending on the weather, the holidays, or the phase of the moon. The head-count on any given day was totally unpredictable, and was not the determining factor of a good time. Seven or eight kids had just as much fun as thirty.

A big game required a larger playing field. Our favorite was the area at the park next to the Field (the Field of the aborted snake hunt). It was not regulation-size, but it was sufficient for munchkin-size kids, which we were. Big kids didn't like this field because the high school field was only a mile away so we usually had it all to ourselves. On the rare occasion when big kids came along wanting it, they simply chased us off. The travails of munchkins.

During the week, Charlie, Pudgy and I mostly played little games on the scraggly traffic circle because there just weren't enough kids in our immediate neighborhood for a big game. But big games were more popular; and we could always count on one on Saturdays when kids seemed to come out of the woodwork, from adjacent neighborhoods, and even from across town.

Big games were the ones we really loved. These were the ones where we got scrapes, bruises, bloody noses, and the occasional broken bone: the Badges of Boyhood.

We had no equipment other than the football, and no uniform other than the clothes on our back. The odd kid that showed up with a helmet or shoulder pads got laughed at.

Big games were what we lived for.

23

AFTER SEVERAL BIG GAMES, an inevitable and good-natured rivalry developed between kids from our neighborhood and kids from the west side of town. One such game became so heated that we decided to have a world championship to sort things out. This suited my purposes perfectly. The more I could keep my friends focused on football, the more likely they were to forget about the snake trick.

Before the rivalry had developed, teams were mixed randomly with kids from all the different neighborhoods. Before each game, team captains were chosen from amongst the better players, and they took turns picking their teammates from the rest of the crowd. As the rivalry matured, teams took on a more neighborhood-oriented bias. The world championship game would formalize that trend. It would be Us versus Them. No equivocation.

This was radical.

This was big.

I was the principal organizer of the team from our neighborhood, Meadowside, and therefore the team captain.

A school chum, named David B Lacey, was the principal organizer and captain of the other team because the game was to be played on a golf driving range owned by his family, called Lacey's Golf Range, located on the west side of town on the Boston Post Road.

To be precise, the game was to be played on a barren patch of ground at the back end of the driving range, behind a sign that read: "300 Yards." This area was considered safe, David B Lacey said, because people rarely hit that far.

The patch of ground was also considered the flattest part of the entire golf range. It was not, however, the softest. Grass fought to survive there, competing with rocks, weeds, and constant abuse from the golf-ball-retrieval contraption, a row of rubber wheels pulled along the ground behind an ancient tractor. The rubber wheels were spaced apart such that golf balls stuck between them and were lifted from the ground by the rotation of the wheels and plopped into a basket. The ancient tractor had an ancient wire cage enclosing an ancient driver. The purpose of the wire cage was two-fold: to protect the ancient driver and to encourage customers to aim balls at the moving tractor. As further inducement to the aiming, a direct hit upon a brass bell affixed to the top of the wire cage earned the lucky customer a free bucket of balls.

The ancient driver was a sprightly octogenarian named Otto, who had driven the tractor since it was new. He was a lively chap for his age, but had, nonetheless, developed a nervous facial tic from twenty years of balls pinging randomly off the wire cage and the bell.

Otto was also a friendly chap, whom Charlie, Pudgy, and I eventually got to know quite well. He loved to regale us with tales of his earlier years, and did so with the genuine enthusiasm of the born story teller. Although not formally schooled, he was street-smart and fashioned the stories for his young audience as would a schoolteacher imparting wisdom. His orations were articulate and instructive, and were punctuated by the tic but never suffered for it. One wonders if the *randomness* of the pings, more than the *sharpness* of the strikes, was the cause of the tic. The question is begged because Otto's tics did not occur at regular intervals, they occurred *at random*.

We were quite fond of Otto. He was kind. His friendliness was manifested in a respectful way, not in the way adults sometimes treat kids as if they're second-class citizens. He always remembered our names, and he insisted we call him Otto, saying he preferred that respect for adults be conveyed by delivery and intention rather than by required utterances, "sir" or "mister."

Driving the tractor was a small part of Otto's duties. Generally speaking, he ran the business. Most of the time, he was up front at the counter renting out balls and clubs. He knew me quite well because I was friends with David B Lacey and we hung around the driving tees together when things were slow. He even let us hit balls out when David B's father wasn't around. We could never get a free soda out of him though because they were kept track of, not like buckets of balls we could fill ourselves and then hit out.

Our usual greeting was, "Yo, Otto, howzit goin'? Can we hit some balls?"

His usual response was, "Yeah, go ahead, but don't **hic** let the old man see ya."

24

DAVID B LACEY NAMED HIS TEAM the "Golf Rangers," for obvious reasons.

There was considerable discussion about a name for our team. We wanted a name that would project the utmost strength and ferocity. Rainbows, or Daffodils, or even Terriers, were out. And names like Pirates, Tigers, and Bears, were already taken. Someone said, Murderers. That sounded good. When we put Murderers together with the name of our neighborhood, Meadowside, alliteration rolled off our lips like sweet cream, so we jumped on it. Thus we became the "Meadowside Murderers." Parents might object, but so what, we figured? We weren't offending any Indian tribe or ethnic group.

On game day, there would typically be thirteen or fourteen players on each side. Not a problem. In these games, everybody played—all at once.

There were no uniforms.
There were no referees.
There were no goal posts.
There were no lines on the field.
There were no coaches.
There were no refreshments.
There were no cheerleaders.
There were no substitutions.
There was no clock.
There was no half-time.
There was no first aid kit.

We didn't care. We had a football; two, as a matter of fact, in case one broke. The rest was superfluous.

I was to start at quarterback for the "Meadowside Murderers." I had six marquis players, the rest were bully-fodder.

Pudgy was our fullback. He was a running refrigerator, a mean momentum machine. When in motion, he was resistant to the state known as *at rest*. He was also an effective blocker because avoiding him was a long way around. He would show up looking crisp and clean, like a runway model, and go home looking like he'd been set upon by a pack of wolves. He was equally comfortable in either condition.

Charlie, although light and rail-thin, was assigned to the tackle position for both offense and defense. He would prefer a more glamorous role, but I needed him in that position because of his unique prowess there. A lineman's job is to repel the opposition, and Charlie was able to perform that task effectively, with minimal contact, courtesy of the detritus adorning his front.

On the interior line, I put the Murphy twins. They were large for their age, not exceptionally bright, but excellent individual athletes when not fighting each other. To keep them apart and focused on the game, I put them on opposite sides of the center.

The center's name was Bobby "YuBang" Gorden, "Yubie," for short. He was a living legend in our neighborhood. He had a withered left leg from Polio, supported by an iron brace. He had an iron will as well, and played baseball and football with the rest of us. His limited mobility made him the obvious candidate for center. He didn't mind. When Yubie ran, which was seldom, he did so with difficulty, lurching and clanking, earning shouts of encouragement rendered exuberantly as in a battle cry: **"On YuBang."** This was not mocking. No indeed. It was an honest endearment that originated one day in a baseball game after Yubie hit a fly ball and was shuffling and rattling to first base.

Yubie's batting stance was dictated by the ravages of his disease. Although he was naturally right-handed, he could not bat righty. Were he to try, his shortened left leg would face the pitcher tilting his upper body forward, forcing an impossibly awkward swing, downward. Of necessity, he hit lefty, withered leg to the rear. The off-kilter stance angled his arms and shoulders backwards, to such extent that the tip of his bat, when drawn back in preparation for the swing, almost touched the ground. His torso, compensating in growth for the lack thereof in the left leg, was disproportionately large, uncommonly strong, and produced a powerful upward swing, the result of which, invariably, was a towering fly-ball to shallow right field, so high it was not easily caught. The odds of a dropped ball and a base hit were about fifty-fifty. When there were enough players, a pinch-runner stood on the opposite side of the plate and ran for Yubie, thus improving the odds of a base hit. When there were insufficient players for that purpose, Yubie ran for himself. This he preferred, although teammates preferred the faster pinch-runner. It was, however, *always* Yubie's call whether to run for himself. That call was sacrosanct. And when he did, **"On YuBang"** resounded with raucous enthusiasm and profound respect.

We had one good candidate to play end, a slightly older kid named Doug Shanahan, who towered over everyone else on the field and could be counted on for dirty tricks.

David B Lacey was quarterback for the "Golf Rangers." At that position, he was adequate, but not great, same as me. He had five marquis players.

Meatloaf Mandalak, second to Charlie in cleanliness and second to none in ruthlessness, was a tall chubby kid with acne. His clothes were always several sizes too large and billowed wildly around him as if his underwear had detonated. A notoriously slow runner—from *our* neighborhood—he had jumped ship and was their fullback. They could have him. He was so unpopular that no one ever cared enough to learn his real name. Meatloaf described him perfectly, so that was the only name he had.

Joey Delvecchio, a mercurial Italian kid, built like a walnut, was their halfback. He was their ringer. He was fast and shifty, perfect for the position. He was also insanely intolerant of hearing his ethnicity impugned. At the sound of the slightest pejorative utterance, no matter how innocuous or humorously intended, he would fly into a rage and blindly attack the presumed source. This propensity was known universally, was ordained to occur in every game, and was eagerly awaited by everyone in attendance. Some things are comforting when you can count on them.

On the interior line, were Socket Hair's two pals, Iggy and the other kid. We had heard rumors that Iggy and the other kid were considered slow learners at school and small-time bullies in the schoolyard. Our personal experience confirmed the usual inaccuracy of rumors: *considered* was not the corrrect word. Since we were seeing more of Iggy and the other kid—and still had no clue what the other kid's name was—we decided to call the other kid Piggy, and not just because it rhymed with Iggy. We also decided that since Iggy and Piggy were eerily inseparable, like conjoined twins, we would use one name when referring to them collectively: Iggy-Piggy.

Playing end—to our disgust and to his delight—was Socket Hair. He wore a knit cap to hide the egg on his forehead, a dirty sweatshirt, and a malevolent grin. Somehow he had found out about the game and had offered his services to the enemy, as, of course, had his retainers, Iggy-Piggy. David B Lacey was unaware of our ongoing war with them, so he gladly accepted their offer. We could hardly blame an honest captain for putting together a competitive team.

With the exception of David B Lacey, these were adversaries to hate.

The game was to be played next Saturday morning.

25

ON FRIDAY BEFORE THE BIG GAME, Charlie ran away from home.

I learned this when I went to his house that afternoon to see if he could come out to play. His mother showed me a note he had left that read: "going to CatMandoo, love Charlie." She said she *wasn't* particularly concerned because he had done this a few times before, and he always came home eventually.

I *was* particularly concerned, about the *eventually* part, because we needed him for the big game tomorrow. I feared that even if he came home tonight, his mother might ground him for tomorrow, so I needed to find him and get him home before it was too late.

His bike was not under the back porch, where only he stashed it, so I knew he had taken it. That told me he probably had gone to the railroad station, which was in town, too far away to walk. Whenever we went to town we rode our bikes. This was another thing I was not allowed to do, but I could get away with it, unless I got killed or came home with my shoes wet.

I figured Charlie had gone to the railroad station because we had discussed running away several times, the way kids do after a spanking or a grounding, and he told me the railroad station was the only place where there was a platform high enough to hop a freight. Apparently, he viewed rail travel as the first step in a journey to the other side of the planet. Even this was somewhat problematical, because freight trains never stopped at our small station, only passenger trains did. I had never pointed that out to Charlie because I didn't want to dampen his enthusiasm. Now it was a stroke of luck that I hadn't because, otherwise, he wouldn't be there waiting for a freight train, and then I wouldn't know where to look for him.

I pedaled into town as fast as I could. Sure enough, there was Charlie, crouching under the platform at the railroad station. I could see him from a block away as I approached on my bike. As I drew closer, I yelled out, "Charlie! Charlie!"

He took one look at me, jumped up on the platform, and ran into the station.

Inside the station, Stationmaster Wendell P Whippoorwill, a dour septuagenarian who had keen eyesight and poor hearing, was chatting flirtatiously with an elderly, multi-layered behemoth of the opposite sex who had equally keen eyesight and equally poor hearing. She was seated holding a white poodle in her lap and he was standing before her at that minimal distance necessary and comfortable only to the mutually hearing-impaired. The most extraordinary aspect of this intercourse was that neither party's exceptional eyesight caused either to recoil in repugnance at the extraordinary homeliness of the other. Either of these two uglies, standing alone, would frighten a totem pole. When seen together, they made your eyes water. Nature prefers symmetry and seeks to match like kinds—lean with lean, tall with tall, etc.—and could prove the point convincingly by matching these poor souls.

The multi-layered behemoth, who called herself Countess Abigail Fensterwald, was waiting for the 3:02 PM train to New York City, which she took there once a month to shop for more layers.

"**Whaddya say we get together when you get back, Abby, maybe go dancing?**" bellowed Wendell P Whippoorwill in her ear.

"**What?**" she screamed.

Before Wendell P could repeat himself, Charlie raced by and tripped over Countess Fensterwald's feet, which had been protruding carelessly from under numerous layers of violet fabric. The Countess lurched at the impact and the poodle jumped off her lap and headed for the door.

Charlie stumbled forward, got his feet under him, realized what he had caused, and impulsively attempted to be of gentlemanly assistance. Completely forgetting why he had been running through the train station, he changed course and took off after the dog.

"**COME BACK, HORSE-SHIT,**" cried Countess Abigail Fensterwald, as Charlie and the poodle raced through the doorway leading out to the waiting platform.

Charlie thought she was calling him, and quickly decided that returning to face the angry behemoth was not in his best interest, so he kept running. He was wise to do so because she was, in fact, calling the dog, not him.

The poodle's name was "Ohrschicht." That was what she had attempted to render. The Countess had named the dog after the given name of her deceased husband, a minor Bavarian count, from whom she had acquired her title. In the small mountain village of the husband's birth, Ohrschicht was pronounced "oar-shhicked," with a guttural *sshhh* and an abrupt *icked*, in classic Germanic fashion. The Countess Fensterwald, nee Abigail Pennybacker, also from a small village—hers being Cuyahoga Falls, Ohio—had been minimally schooled, and was not adept in foreign languages. Try as she might to properly annunciate *Ohrschicht*, it came out, *Horse-shit*. This was understandable, given that due to her hearing impairment, she had never heard Ohrschicht pronounced correctly in the first place, nor had she ever heard it bastardized by herself in the second place.

26

THE MINOR BAVARIAN COUNT, Ohrschicht Fensterwald, stood six feet and nine inches tall in his stocking feet. Almost as wide, he was a portrait of his Teutonic heritage. His substantial height was genetic. His substantial girth was not. Owing to beer, bratwurst and Bavarian strudel, which he consumed in copious quantities even as his coronary arteries shrank to mere pinholes, he was, nevertheless, as big as an Alaskan Brown Bear.

He was an only-child, unmarried, and had read for a graduate degree in world history at the prestigious Ludwig-Maximilians-Universitat in Munich. While at university, he began to tinker with a small nest-egg of funds given him by his father to invest for his own account. Father had provided these funds as a means of distracting the young count from constantly interfering in the family business. In hindsight, father should have encouraged the interference. The young count's financial acumen proved far superior to that of the family's best advisers. Over the years he parlayed the small nest-egg into a sizable fortune—all his own.

He was thirty-eight years old in March of 1933, residing in comfortable apartments in Munich, enjoying a life of leisure, when the Reichstag went up in flames. The Nazis blamed the fire on the Communists and Socialists, and he took notice. He was neither politically active, nor politically naïve, and although he held no public office, it was known in social circles that he preferred ideologies left of center. In July of that same year, Germany became a one-party state, and its civil service and judiciary were purged of non-Aryans and leftists. This time he viewed events rightly; dark storm clouds, foreboding and irreversible, were gathering over his homeland. With alarm and alacrity, he began an orderly process of liquidating his assets and transferring the proceeds out of the country. He was, by now, and by necessity, immeasurably adept in facilitating financial transactions, in the way of one who has obtained wealth by industry rather than inheritance. Needing no textbook for guidance, he carefully transferred his funds in small increments, spacing them randomly over a period of five years, thereby skillfully avoiding the attention of authorities, thinking to himself the entire time, "Humph, Master Race, indeed."

One day, in 1938, as he sat in a Zurich café celebrating the successful transfer of the last increment of his fortune into a Swiss bank, he learned of Adolph Hitler's annexation of Austria. By the time he finished his cognac, he had made the wise decision to remain right where he was, in this convenient country with the resolute determination and unfathomable ability to remain neutral.

He lived in Switzerland in relative obscurity during the war years, keeping his own counsel, husbanding his investments, and lamenting the historical stains that would mark the country of his birth for all eternity.

In 1947, the war over, his fortune largely intact, he booked passage on the Queen Mary, moved himself and his fortune to New York City, and took up residence in the Dakota, a sumptuous apartment building on the corner of 72nd Street and Central Park West. There, he rekindled his scholarly juices, and studied the Constitution of the United States from dawn to dusk. A year later, he became a naturalized citizen.

Eventually, he met Miss Abigail Pennybacker, a stout farm girl from Cuyahoga Falls, Ohio, possessed of a quick wit and a pleasant temperament. She had come to New York City before the war to experience a wider view of the world, and had secured employment as an executive secretary at RCA, the famous *Radio Corporation of America*, in Rockefeller Center, the city's most prestigious business address. The job and its address marked a propitious beginning, and she prepared to commence her new life with enthusiasm. Sadly, the war broke out, and her plan for a wider view of the world languished in the confines of a drab apartment, and a dull job. She toiled unhappily and unfulfilled for six years until a chance introduction to a minor Bavarian count revived her hope for the wider view. With companionship as an additional objective, she visited her feminine wiles upon the Count with a vengeance. The Count responded eagerly, absorbing her attentions like a dry sponge thrown in a bathtub, for he, too, yearned for companionship. They formed an immediate and inseparable bond. They walked together in Central Park, read together at the New York Public Library, and skated together at Rockefeller Center. They attended the openings of the best Broadway plays and sampled the cuisine of the best uptown restaurants. They were happy as pigs in mud.

In the classic tradition of European royalty, Count Ohrschicht Fensterwald courted Miss Abigail Pennybacker, formally, for three years.

It is understandable that the count adored Miss Pennybacker's immense girth, given the immensity of his own. It is inexplicable, however, why he adored her singular homeliness. He was, after all, rather handsome, in the aristocratic way of his lineage. She was, on the other hand, homelier than a Colobus monkey, in the corn-fed way of hers. *Blindly in love* comes to mind. Or desparate. The rationale was irrelevant. He was immensely content, for the first time in his life. He accepted all of her *as is* (no mean task), including her inadequacies with the German language, which tacitly encouraged her mispronunciations. She never called him by his first name, preferring to address him formally as "my dear Count," so he had never heard her unique rendering of Ohrschicht. Had he lived to hear it, he would have been amused to distraction by the expression on the faces of "polite company" when the question of the dog's name arose and the prim Countess Abigail Fensterwald, believing she had mastered the Bavarian dialect, belted out an ear-splitting, **"Horse-shit."**

27

IN THE SUMMER OF 1950, Count Ohrschicht Fensterwald, formerly of Bavaria, and Miss Abigail Pennybacker, formerly of Ohio, married in a civil ceremony in New York City, attended by a small group of close friends. After a brief reception at a small downtown hotel, they headed into Connecticut, along the Merritt Parkway, towards New Haven, in a brand new Packard Super Deluxe 8 Sedan the size of an ocean liner, purchased especially for the occasion.

The Count was a good chap, who respected the country of his wife's birth with the special enthusiasm of a naturalized citizen. He had, therefore, suggested that their honeymoon should be a motor tour through the New England states to trace the history of the country's birth. Abigail Pennybacker had never ventured beyond Cuyahoga Falls or the concrete walls of New York City, so she embraced his suggestion as if it were her own.

Less than an hour after leaving New York, they crossed the Housatonic River, paid the Milford toll, exited the Merritt Parkway, and continued towards the center of town via the famous and historic Boston Post Road. After less than a mile, the Count was pleasantly surprised to find, on the right-hand side of the road, a quaint golf driving range, called Lacey's Golf Range. He politely *asked* permission of his new bride (they were on their honeymoon after all) if they might make a wee stop there, so he could hit out just one little bucket of balls. He was, he explained, an avid golfer, who rarely had sufficient opportunity to enjoy that sport. Eagerly wishing their marriage to get off on a high note, the newly-minted Countess responded lovingly, "By all means, my dear Count, do hit a few balls."

So they stopped, and he did, sweating profusely in the hot afternoon sun, blood pressure soaring.

Upon departing the golf driving range, he gave a generous tip to the little old man at the counter with the facial tic and "Otto" embroidered on his shirt, and bowed formally with a, "Thank you, kind sir."

The Count was a proud and happy man.

Back in the Packard Super Deluxe 8 Sedan, they continued the journey to their originally intended first stop, an historic site in the center of Milford town. There, the Count was keen to have a quick look at Bushnell's Turtle, the first submarine used by American military forces against a foreign warship.

Built by David Bushnell in 1776, the tiny rusted hulk of Bushnell's Turtle was a neglected relic of the Revolutionary War. It stood alone and untended, on a dusty field, at the end of the town's picturesque harbor. Townspeople ignored it. Historians and Revolutionary War scholars revered it. Count Fensterwald worshipped it.

It was late-afternoon, still sweltering, by the time Count Ohrschicht Fensterwald parked his new Packard on the dusty field, next to Bushnell's Turtle. In less than an hour, he would be checking into the Bridal Suite at the Howard Johnson's Motor Lodge, and shortly thereafter, he would be consummating the only marriage of a long and tedious life. Finally appreciating a sense of urgency, he hove his immense bulk out of the front seat of the car, wiped his brow with a handkerchief, motioned to his new bride to wait in the car for he would only be a minute, hastened over to Bushnell's Turtle, reached out reverently to touch it—just once—and within a tiny inch of doing so, dropped over dead from an acute myocardial infarction.

Ironically, in the almost-200-year history of the submarine that spawned a new chapter in the nation's development of military weaponry, the good Count Ohrschicht Fensterwald of Bavaria, an erudite historian, a decent chap, not an enemy combatant, was its first victim.

28

THE NEW WIDOW, Countess Fensterwald, too unfamiliar with romance to be utterly devastated, considered this turn of events pragmatically. She ran the facts of her initial good fortune and subsequent misfortune around in her head until she had reached conclusions and a plan.

She had left Cuyahoga Falls as a penniless maiden, so she could not possibly return there as a wealthy widow, a Lady preferring the stable to the manor house.

She certainly could not descend upon a small village in Bavaria, where she was not known, did not speak the language, and would not be received by the Count's family, an eight-hour Countess bearing their name and holding his fortune.

And she quickly dismissed the notion of returning to New York City to find another husband, recognizing that her match with the good Count was a one-off. The likelihood of meeting another wealthy, titled gentleman the size of a bear was not even slim, it was none. She accepted that, a conclusion made easier by the testate devise (his idea, not hers) of a sizable fortune, and made the oddly romantic decision to settle there, in the pleasant little New England town with the picturesque harbor and the Bushnell's Turtle, where she could fashion any sort of tale regarding the origin of her title, and get a white poodle for companionship. That was two years ago.

Here she was now, in the railroad station of the pleasant little New England town, with a white poodle named Ohrschicht, entertaining the amorous intentions of a potential mate (against all odds), and in a state of extreme distress.

29

AS I PULLED UP to the station and hopped off my bike, a white poodle emerged from the station, chased by Charlie, whose good offices were increasing rather than diminishing the dog's panic.

Ohrschicht shot straight across the waiting platform, and took flight where the platform ended and the narrow canyon of railroad tracks began.

Countess Fensterwald burst from the station doorway in the very next instant, which happened to be the very same instant that the Boston Express whizzed by breaking the sound barrier. She watched in horror as the headlight of the train's locomotive intercepted Ohrschicht dead on.

It happened so fast, there wasn't even a *splat* sound.

Countess Fensterwald fainted, and melted onto the platform in a pool of fatness and flounce.

Wendell P Whippoorwill hobbled out, brought her to, and tried lamely to comfort her. He fanned her face with his hand, and bellowed in her ear, **"I'll call Boston and ask if they can scrape the remains off the locomotive, Abby, so you can have a proper burial."** Wendell was a smoothy.

"WAAAAA," she cried. **"MY HORSE-SHIITTT."**

Charlie was just standing there, inert, a vacant expression on his face. Then he laughed hysterically, and all eyes turned on him.

"Charlie! Charlie!" I yelled, for the second time in the last thirty seconds, and all eyes turned on me.

Charlie looked at me, looked at Wendell, looked at the supine Countess, then remembered he was supposed to be running away, and took off like a shot.

I chased him all around downtown for half an hour, until he got tired and I was able to cut him off on the village green and throw a body block that knocked him down. I grabbed a leg and we rolled around on the ground as he tried to wriggle out of my grasp. I held tight.

"Cut it out Charlie," I said. "You didn't even tell that lady you were sorry for killing her dog."

"What for? I didn't kill him, the train did. Wasn't my fault. I was just trying to help. Lemme go."

"Not unless you come home. We need you for the big game tomorrow."

"I'm going to Catmandoo," he said, still struggling.

"Go after the game," I said, still holding on.

"I gotta keep going. I can't go home now, my mom'll kill me."

"Not if you go home right now she won't."

"No, no, I gotta go," he said.

"Besides, you can't go back to the station and hang around waiting for a freight train. The cops'll be there."

"They won't catch me," he said, remaining obstinate.

This left me with no other choice but to shoot my silver bullet.

"Okay," I said. "You can play quarterback."

His eyes widened. He hadn't thought of that. I could tell from the way his eyes lit up that he hadn't been holding out on me just for that. He honestly hadn't thought about it.

"Quarterback?" he said.

"Yeah."

"Really?"

"Yeah, if we go now, before it gets too late and your mother grounds you," I said.

"Okay."

I let go.

Everybody wants to play quarterback. It has a power of its own.

We ran back to the station, sneaked around the platform, found our bikes, and beat it on home. That was the end of running away—for now.

30

THE NEXT DAY WAS SATURDAY. The game started about 10:00 AM. It was mildly overcast but clear. No rain.

The playing field had been swept earlier in the day by Otto, who declared it to be "ball-**hic**-free," but there were still a few balls on the ground that Otto's contraption had missed. These we threw aside.

The teams lined up, facing each other.

There was some jostling, name calling, and the ordinary fighting words.

"Gonna kick yer ass," from Socket Hair.

"Eat me," from Yubie.

We were visitors, so they kicked off.

Pudgy took the kick off and headed straight up the middle, bowling over a couple Golf Rangers before Meatloaf Mandalak clotheslined him. He went down hard.

Iggy-Piggy piled on.

The Murphy twins ran over and piled onto Iggy-Piggy.

Charlie, who never smelled like a rose himself, approached the pile from downwind and caught the stench coming off of Piggy. He hesitated for a fraction of a second, made a face, ran around to the upwind side, and piled on.

Two smaller Golf Rangers, ragamuffins in short pants I'd never seen before—one missing a few teeth, the other missing a few marbles—looked on tentatively for all of two seconds, gave a rebel yell, and piled on themselves.

Joey Delvecchio felt left out, so he piled on too.

The mountain of bodies writhed and squirmed like a pile of worms.

Then Charlie found a limb in the pile and bit into it. It was Joey Delvecchio's leg. Joey screamed, and kicked Charlie in the face. The kick did not dislodge any teeth, so Charlie bit him again. Joey jerked his leg back and the pile quivered.

Socket Hair ran over and elbowed Pudgy trying to squirm up out of the pile. Pudgy fell back into it. Doug Shanahan came to Pudgy's defense by way of kicking Socket Hair in the nuts. Socket Hair fell over and rolled on the ground in a fetal position, holding his crotch and moaning. He was a magnet for pain.

Yubie jumped on Meatloaf's back.

A fight ensued.

David B Lacey and I watched in amusement, delighted at what we had wrought. It was the perfect start to a glorious game.

"All right, all right, that's enough!" I yelled, as David B Lacey and I pulled our boys out of the pile.

Eventually, everyone cooled down and the game began in earnest. After a few series, patterns formed, plays developed, and scoring began. The game rolled on, both teams scoring at will. Perfect football.

But not without further incident.

Joey Delvecchio was earning distinction as the leading scorer for the Golf Rangers when Doug Shanahan called him "Whoppo."

"Yippee!" Charlie yelled. "Here we go."

"You sonofabitch!" cried Joey. He fumed until his face was crimson red and his head looked like it would explode. He shook all over like he had the shivers, then dove blindly at Doug Shanahan, determined to tear him to shreds. Doug stepped aside like a toreador and brushed him off. He tried again. Doug brushed him off again. After a few more tries, he abandoned the worthless tactic and returned to his position on the field. But he wasn't done yet. When the game resumed he commenced a policy of body-blocking Doug Shanahan on every play, offensive or defensive, with such maniacal intensity that both of them became ineffective as scorers. Doug was not one of our principal scorers so the altercation became a factor in our favor.

Joey Delvecchio's obsession with Doug Shanahan kept Joey from blitzing our quarterback. Charlie was then able to enjoy his new position largely unchallenged. After a few series, his arm got hot; he threw Pudgy and me a few touchdowns, and even ran for a couple himself.

Socket Hair got frustrated and began elbowing opposing players at the snap of the ball, claiming it a legal blocking technique. In response, we quadruple-teamed him with four of our dirtiest players, a propitious use of extras one might otherwise be reluctant to employ.

The Murphy twins and Iggy-Piggy settled into a conveniently symmetrical contest that had more to do with injury and incapacitation than with blocking and tackling. Some blood was let, none of it in anger.

Meatloaf Mandalak continued to employ his signature clothesline maneuver, until he blindsided Charlie with one and Charlie returned the favor with a ferocity that nearly decapitated him.

Oddly, even the dirtiest of the Golf Rangers respected Yubie's limitation, and treated him with kid gloves until we pulled the old fumble-roosky gag and Yubie scored to a rousing chorus of, **"On YuBang."**

After that, Yubie was fair game and he took his share of hits. In truth, he rather enjoyed being treated equally. Of course, the acquisition of a new target was welcome news to the Golf Rangers.

The game continued in this fashion for the remainder of the day.

At some point in the middle of the afternoon, Janie and Mary Lou showed up with the announced purpose of checking to see if there really was a big game and who might be playing in it. But Mary Lou wasn't fooling me. Although she affected no demonstrable evidence she even knew I was there, I knew she had really come to see me play. I knew what nobody else knew because the evidence was demonstrable only to me. It was in the way she was standing, in those tight pedal-pushers, preparing to flash her signature pose. I knew that's what she was up to. I could sense it. She was challenging me to look over, to risk distraction for a peek.

Sure enough, as I was going deep for a pass, down her side of the field, she pulled her clever little ploy. Smirking coyly, shifting her weight onto one leg, angling her body sideways, she pointed her butt in my direction. There was no force of nature that could prevent me from looking over at that tight little butt. She knew it. I knew it.

I was in full stride, a very cool full stride, a fancy prancing full stride, arms outstretched to receive the ball hurdling in my direction, thence to execute a dazzling scamper across the goal line for a showboat touchdown, when I looked over.

The pass from Charlie was a rocket. It hit me in the back of the head. I fell down, face first, in the dirt, at Mary Lou's feet.

"Damn!" I growled at the dirt.

I stayed face-down for a few moments, trying to gather my composure. I thought, perhaps if I leap to my feet unruffled and valiantly return to the game she would think that cool.

Then I felt a wet tear hit my cheek. And another.

What? She's crying? For me? Crying in alarm? She fears I might be hurt? My heart surged with joy.

Then more tears. A torrent of tears.

I was dumb to everything happening around me, such was my joy. I looked up to reassure her I was okay.

She was bent over, her face next to mine, weeping hysterically, uncontrollably, showering me with crocodile tears—of laughter.

I became aware that there was other laughter too, coming from everybody else on the field. But I didn't hear that laughter; I only heard ... hers.

The remainder of humanity was unmoved by this drama I thought a tragedy but was merely a farce.

I don't remember what happened next, other than the game seemed to resume itself magically and I found myself on the far side of the field trying to shrink to the size of a pea.

Janie and Mary Lou watched the game for a few more minutes, doing what they were doing before I made a fool of myself, which is exhibiting no interest whatsoever in the outcome of the game and calling out no words of encouragement.

The game continued without my full attention. Charlie threw a spectacular touchdown pass to Pudgy and began strutting like a peacock, looking over at Janie with the *uh-huh-that's-right* expression on his face, hoping to impress her. Both of Charlie's eyes had focused perfectly during his execution of the play, but, in the celebratory aftermath, only the good eye fixed solidly on Janie while the other danced around inside its socket like a marble in a glass jar. Janie turned to face Mary Lou and they made a grimacing gesture to each other. Then they huddled together and laughed conspiratorially. I felt sorry for Charlie. He had a good heart in spite of his outward appearance. He was just a little too rough around the edges for the likes of Janie Wagner. No genie in a bottle could reverse Janie's predisposition when it came to Charlie. You can't un-bake a cake.

I reflected on this situation. I was no better off than Charlie. My success rate with the opposite sex was no better than Charlie's. I was a little too rough around the edges for Mary Lou. It was a dispiriting revelation. But she was so pretty I couldn't help dreaming. And she was only ten. Imagine, I thought, when she grows up? I was too young to find consolation in a sad truth: the darlings of ten, very often, end up the dogs of twenty. And vice versa.

The game continued. I looked about to re-orient myself and saw that Socket Hair was taking notice of the girls. "This oughta be good," I said to no one in particular, as he started flashing lewd gestures in their direction. At first, they paid no attention to him. But when he kept it up, they feigned indignation, wheeled about, and left without a word. "Serves them right," I thought, bitterly.

Along about 4:00, as it began to get dark, kids started melting away and heading home.

The game finally ended about 5:00. There were only eight players left, four on each side. There were not eight kids on the planet more content. There were not any filthier either.

There had been so many incidents, fouls, fights, injuries, times out, and plays called back, that a mathematician with a slide rule and an abacus could not have determined the final score. We never knew, and we didn't care.

Only two players had gotten hit by golf balls. Somewhere around noon, Meatloaf Mandalak took a bouncer to the ankle and limped around for awhile to get sympathy. He incurred no discernable damage and soon returned to the game with his lightning-quick form undiminished. Socket Hair got beaned an hour later and sat on the sidelines for ten minutes massaging another lump on his head. Nobody could tell if he incurred *any* damage, and nobody inquired since the injury was only to his head. Eventually, he returned to the game without missing a beat. Later on, Iggy fell on a golf ball and bruised his ego.

For poetic justice, golf balls had made contact only with Golf Rangers, the worst of which was with Socket Hair.

Charlie was voted MVP of our team, and announced that he would not run away again, as long as he could play quarterback.

Pudgy looked like he'd been keelhauled. He was never happier.

I was filthy from head to toe. My face was scratched, my pants were torn, and my sweatshirt was bloody. I wasn't worried, because my mother wouldn't care about the condition of my face or clothes. My shoes were not wet.

31

THE BUZZ IN THE NEIGHBORHOOD the next week was about the world championship football game. I tried to keep that subject on front burner so that my failed attempt to find a snake to throw at my mother would become a distant memory.

But I was only fooling myself. I had made such a big deal of it, parading by Janie and Mary Lou, shooting off my big mouth, that Charlie and Pudgy could never forget it.

Monday, nothing.

Tuesday, nothing. Sweet quiet. I might make it.

Wednesday, "Hey, let's go find that snake now," *shouted* Charlie, within earshot of Pudgy.

"Shit!" I mumbled. I tried to change the subject. "How 'bout that fumble-roosky? Was that cool, or what?"

"How 'bout that snake gag?" said Charlie.

"Yeah?" chimed in Pudgy.

"Shit!"

These were my best friends, calling my manhood (boyhood?) into question. And for good reason, I was always trying to weasel out of it.

I had no choice.

"Okay, okay, tomorrow," I said, as one stupid last chance, hoping that tomorrow they would forget. Fat chance.

Thursday, I avoided all the usual places. That worked until about 3:00, when Charlie and Pudgy found me trying to be invisible.

"Okay, ready now?" said Charlie.

Pudgy was grinning like a Cheshire cat. I wanted to slap him.

"Shit! I said for the umpteenth time. "Okay, let's go."

So back we went, past Janie's house, quietly this time, sheepishly, my head hung low. They knew. I knew. Pudgy and Charlie knew. I didn't need to dig myself deeper in the hole.

We got to the Field. It was a cool day, but I was sweating anyway. No more excuses.

I found my forked stick and started poking around.

Silently, I repeated my entreaty to the Gods to rid the Field of serpents.

But the Gods were against me this day. They knew poetic justice, or rather it was their Specialty. As proof they dislodged a mighty serpent from beneath a pile of leaves.

I jumped.

My heart skipped a beat and my head spun at the sight of the odious beast.

What I *saw,* was a demon from Hell, an angry viper from the depths of the inferno.

What it *was,* was a harmless 18-inch long garter snake, half an inch in diameter, more scared of me than I of it (to the extent such were possible).

The snake slithered off through the weeds. There was a lot of running around, falsetto screaming, "There he is, there he is," that sort of thing.

"Eeeeehhh!" Charlie began roaring, jumping up and down, spinning frantically in circles, scattering flies from his shoes and snot from his nose.

"Get'im!" Pudgy squeeled.

"You get'im," I barked.

"No, no, no, it's your idea," he shot back. "You get'im."

"Okay, okay, okay."

I chased the snake through the weeds, ready at last to pin it down with the forked stick.

"Hey, what are you guys doing?" came a loud shout from across the street.

I looked up, startled.

Socket Hair and Iggy-Piggy were crossing the street, heading our way. Socket Hair had a stick or branch in his hand and was waving it about menacingly. Apparently, Pudgy's lessons had not had the desired affect.

I looked down in the weeds.

The snake was gone.

At that point, it seemed like being gone was a good thing for the three of us to be as well.

I dropped the forked stick, and we took off running in the opposite direction as fast as we could. I had failed to find a snake again, but that was not my principal concern at the moment. No act of bravery, no saving of face, was worth sticking around for.

We headed for Old Man Kramer's house and the short cut through his yard to the hole in the fence into Charlie's yard.

Old Man Kramer was puttering around in his garden as we came around the corner of his house at full tilt. Ordinarily we checked to make sure he wasn't around before we ran through his yard, but this was an unanticipated emergency so we threw caution to the wind and dashed through it anyway.

Apparently Old Man Kramer wasn't as asleep at the switch as we thought. He was standing there bright-eyed as if we had an appointment with him. He smiled warmly, waved a friendly greeting, and motioned us on. I thought this quite odd until we got closer to the fence and saw that he had nailed the slats back up.

By now he was laughing uncontrollably, unaware that three pursuers were right behind us and would soon round the corner of his house and make their appearance.

We couldn't blame Old Man Kramer for closing up the hole in the fence. After all, it was his fence. He was a nice old guy, really—proprietary perhaps, but never mean-spirited. He was just having himself a good yuck, thinking he put one over on us. In this, he was being generous. He could have ratted us out to our parents but he didn't; he just nailed the slats back up and tried to make a good gag out of it.

Unfortunately, the laugh would be on him. He didn't know he was messing with the Short-Cut Kings. We didn't earn that distinction by being stupid—unlike our pursuers. Short-cuts were our life. Most grownups were averse to short-cuts, and their mean side demanded that they frustrate their use, block them, seal them off, nail them shut, make them higher. We appreciated attempts to thwart our short-cutting, and so to counter them we had developed special maneuvers, one of which we now employed.

Without breaking stride, I yelled, "Charlie, we'll make *The Steps*, Pudgy, you're last." No elaboration was needed.

I slowed and let Charlie reach the fence first. He bent over at the waste and made his back the top step. I stopped in front of Charlie, dropped down on all fours, and made my back the bottom step. A split-second behind, Pudgy pranced up the two steps with an agility honed chasing butterflies, rolled over the top of the fence, and landed in Charlie's yard as graceful as a ballet dancer. In the next split-second, Charlie and I jumped up, grabbed the top of the fence, and hoisted ourselves up and over.

After a good laugh, we stuck our heads up over the fence and made faces at our pursuers, who had stopped next to Old Man Kramer standing there in his garden.

"Well, I'll be damned," muttered Old Man Kramer. He was confounded at first, until he turned and noticed Socket Hair and Iggy-Piggy standing next to him, an arms-length away, looking as perplexed as he was. It took him a few seconds to gather his wits, and a few more to process the picture of a filthy dimwit with greasy red hair picking his nose, a cyclopean gnome with too many teeth grimacing vacantly, and a fetid midget with one tooth trying to work his tongue around it and into a nostril—a trio of circus freaks radiating the collective intelligence of 1.5 woodchucks. He blinked a few times hoping that blinking would make the picture go away, and when he realized it wouldn't, he waved his hoe at them and shouted, **"Get out of here! Whatever you've got, I don't wanna catch it."**

Socket Hair and Iggy-Piggy were startled by this outburst, but not so badly that their feet froze to the ground. They ran out of the yard, with Old Man Kramer half-heartedly trailing after them, and stopped in the middle of the street. Old Man Kramer stopped in his driveway, waved the hoe at them, then turned around quickly so they couldn't see the grin on his face and ambled back to his garden.

Like drunkards tossed from a bar, they milled around in the street for a few minutes, trying to figure out their next move. After a brief conversation that surely exhausted their planning skills, they called to us to come out.

We didn't.

Instead, we cowered behind Charlie's back porch and made more faces at them.

They stood there for a few minutes, waving their fists and leering at us. Finally, they realized we weren't coming out, so they gave up, and went back in the direction of the Field to find someone else to intimidate.

This time I had a legitimate reprieve. It felt great.

32

IT WAS OBVIOUS that Socket Hair had not been dissuaded by Pudgy's lessons. Perhaps we had even made things worse. He knew that Charlie and I had been involved with Pudgy somehow, and so now he wanted to make trouble for all three of us. And it looked like he was not going to be caught alone again. He had his trusty retainers, Iggy-Piggy, with him everywhere he went. It was shaping up to be a gang war.

It seemed there was no end to his vengeance.

We needed another plan.

Otto was sitting behind the counter at Lacey's Golf Range reading a newspaper when I arrived. He had swept the field of balls earlier, and was now waiting for customers. It was late morning and there were none yet. He perked up when he saw me, and waited for my usual greeting.

Instead, I said, "Otto, we got a problem."

"Who's we?"

"Me and Charlie and Pudgy."

"What's **hic** the problem?"

I told him the whole story, starting with the first day we had met Pudgy in the schoolyard, and ending the day before when Socket Hair and Iggy-Piggy had chased us from the Field.

"They're gunning for all of us now, not just Pudgy," I said.

"Well, it looks like you pissed in the soup, eh?" he said, slightly mixing the metaphor.

"Whaddya mean?" I said.

"I mean, you guys tried to solve a problem, and all youse did was make matters worse. Right?"

"Yeah, I guess."

"Guess, my ass. That's exactly what you did."

"Yeah, you're right. That's why we got a problem."

Otto didn't say a word. He just sat back and smiled.

I smiled back.

He smiled more brightly, clearly amused.

My smile hung by a thread; I was scared.

We sat there like that for awhile, each waiting for the other to recommence the conversation. He wasn't being mean. He knew what I came for, he just wanted *me* to say it.

Finally, I said, "What're we gonna do?"

He scratched his head, made a **hic** sound, juggled a couple golf balls, smiled some more, and said, "Well, you guys certainly can't engage them directly, right?"

"*Engage, directly,* what's that mean?"

"Means *make contact.* Means you can't fight'em physically, face to face. Means you gotta fight 'em with smarts, not with fists."

"Ain't that what got us in this trouble in the first place?"

"Maybe, **hic** maybe not. Maybe you just gotta be smarter next time."

So, therein commenced another period of silence and smiling.

After a few minutes, when I couldn't stand it any longer, I said, "Otto, we know what we *can't* do; we need to figure out what we *can* do."

"Right you are, Sonny Boy," he said, enjoying every bit of the squirming and fidgeting I was doing.

"So you got any ideas?"

"Okay, okay, hmm, maybe you could try an illusion."

"What's a *lusion*?"

"Like a magic trick. What magicians do when they make a lady disappear. She don't really disappear, the magician makes your eyes think she does. He tricks your eyes. That's an illusion. Same thing like when they make something *appear*, like a ghost or a monster."

"Okay, that's good. How do we make that red-headed kid and his pals disappear?" I said.

"I don't know how to do that. I just know what it is. Besides, it's probably gonna be easier to make something *appear*, rather than *disappear*. Make something frightening appear, scare the shit outa them."

"Okay, so how do we do that?"

"Dunno that either," he said. "I'm just **hic** the idea man."

My visit with Otto was inconclusive. I wasn't sure if I had a plan or not, so I went looking for Charlie and Pudgy to report on the conversation. I found them both in Charlie's backyard watching Old Man Kramer checking that the boards were still nailed on his fence.

"You kids better leave this fence be," he was growling when I arrived. "That goes for you too," he said to me.

"Yessir," I said, not wanting to make unnecessary trouble. We might need his cooperation someday.

Charlie and Pudgy were making faces at old man Kramer when he wasn't looking. I pulled them both aside and told them what Otto said.

"Here we go again," said Pudgy.

"I can make little things disappear," said Charlie, referring to his frog trick, "but I can't blow up a person."

"So all we have is a suggestion from Otto to try some magic tricks that we don't know nothin' about?" said Pudgy.

"That's about it," I said.

"We in trouble," said Charlie.

While we were contemplating our predicament, Charlie's mother came out the back door of the house onto the porch. She saw that we were in quiet contemplation, and then waved politely at Old Man Kramer, apparently delighted with the peace and harmony in the two backyards.

"Anybody want ice cream?" she called to us.

"**Yeeaaa!**" went a chorus of happiness, ending our deliberations for the day.

33

THE NEXT DAY I rounded up Charlie and Pudgy and we went to see Tweedle Dee and Tweedle Dum. Their real names were Ted and Fred, which is what we called them in public. Tweedle Dee and Tweedle Dum were our secret names, reserved for confidential use among the three of us.

They were going into high school next year so they were of an age when ten-year-olds are an amusement and twelve-year-olds a pain in the ass. The fortunate coincidence was that we were ten and Socket Hair had just turned twelve.

Another fortunate coincidence was that Socket Hair had distinguished himself to the brothers by harassing Janie and Mary Lou in the schoolyard, and had compounded the mistake by making lewd gestures at our football game. Janie had promptly reported these events to her brothers. Tweedle Dee and Tweedle Dum did not appreciate the ragged misfit bothering their little sister and her best friend. Consequently, they were pleasantly pre-disposed to entertain our request for assistance in disabusing the misfit of his discourteous ways. They were too old to deal with him directly, so they welcomed the opportunity to sponsor a proxy war.

In contrast to their macabre interest in instruments of capital punishment, Tweedle Dee and Tweedle Dum were ideal students in school, well-liked by their teachers, and respected by their peers. They spent most of their time in the school shop, tinkering with electricity, magnetism and rotating mechanical contrivances. They played no sports.

It was impossible to tell which twin was which because they were absolutely identical, and they intentionally perpetuated the impossibility by playing twin numbers on everyone, including their own siblings. They dressed alike, but that was just the tip of the iceberg. They ate the same foods, exchanged name tags, sat in each other's seat, answered each other's questions, spoke simultaneously on random occasions, and never quarreled. Teachers were totally confused by these tactics, and eventually stopped trying to figure out who was who. It didn't matter who answered whose question, or whose name was on a test or report, because their test scores and grades, earned without collaboration or cheating, were also, and always, identical. It was eerie, but unassailable.

I had no problem communicating with them. It was like talking to one person with double brainpower. It was a kick. I was easily amongst those who respected them.

Their proficiency in mechanical and electrical engineering was what had brought us to this meeting. Their lack of affection for Socket Hair was icing on the cake.

They listened intently as I told them about my conversation with Otto.

"He said we should try to scare them with a lusion."

"A what?" said Fred.

"A lusion."

They looked at each other; two brains thinking in unison. Not many folks got to see this.

"You mean an *illusion*?" both said at once.

"Yeah, that's it," I said.

"Well, that part's easy," said Ted.

"It is?"

"Sure," said Fred, with a conspiratorial look at his brother. "We kinda ... well ... specialize in illusions."

Then Ted said, "But an illusion of what? That's the question. And the overall strategy? That's another question. A bigger one. In other words, what's the plan Stan?"

"Ummh ... well ... we was hoping you could help us with that too," said Pudgy.

"I thought so," said Fred—or Ted.

It was up to us to think the problem through and come back to Tweedle Dee and Tweedle Dum with ideas and suggestions. They were willing to help us out, but not willing to do all the work.

So we repaired to our thinking spot at the creek, where Charlie could sacrifice some living creature and get his thinking juices flowing.

As we were heading there, a large bullfrog with unfortunate timing plunked across the path in front of Charlie.

He grabbed it.

"Oh, this is a beauty! An M-80, an M-80, my shirt for an M-80!" he said, in cadence reminiscent of, "A horse, a horse, my kingdom for a horse."

"Aww, Charlie, look at him. He's scared ... you're so much bigger than him," said Pudgy.

"Yeah, but if I had an M-80, he wouldn't be scared for long. Tick-tock-tick-blooey. Yahoooo!"

"Wait a minute, you guys, that's it," I said.

"What's *it*?" said Pudgy.

"Charlie's size, compared to the frog. He's so big that the frog is scared just looking at him," I said.

"What's that got to do with our problem?" asked Pudgy.

"If we were that much bigger than that red-headed kid and his pals, that would scare the shit outa *them*," I said.

"So how do we get that big?" asked Charlie.

"I dunno. Maybe Tweedle Dee and Tweedle Dum can make a magic pill that makes us bigger, like Alice in Wonderland, or something. Some kinda lusion," I said.

"Let's ask 'em," said Pudgy.

"An Alice in Wonderland pill? Naw, we don't know how to do that," said Ted.

"Besides, you would need another pill to shrink yourself back to normal size, and we don't know how to do that either," said Fred.

"No, I don't need no second pill. I'd just stay big; then my dad wouldn't spank me anymore," said Charlie.

"Be serious, Charlie," said Fred.

Okay, okay."

"So that was a bad idea?" I said.

"Maybe not," said Fred. "Lemme talk to Ted."

"Okay."

They talked. There was a lot of technical jargon we had never heard before, words like *focal length, acoustics, voltage*.

We waited.

It seemed like forever.

We waited some more. We were getting good at waiting. When you've got brains working for free, on your behalf, you wait.

It still seemed like forever.

Finally, they both said, "you were on the right track to begin with, talkin' about bein' bigger and some kind of illusion. We can probably make you *look* bigger. We can make an illusion that you are bigger."

"Whaddya mean?" I said.

"Well, maybe we can make some kind of frightening images, using you guys as the models, and project 'em on a screen or a wall," said Fred. "An image projected on a wall can be gigantic."

"That's what the movies are, projected images," said Ted. "Your images will be still, we can't make moving images, but maybe we can make them appear to be moving by shaking the projector or something."

"But the movies don't scare anyone," said Charlie.

"Oh they do, they do," said Fred. "You ever see how girls scream at a horror movie? With the right images, timing, lighting, and noises, we can scare the shit out of anybody."

"Yeah, really?" I said.

"Yeah."
"Cool!" said Charlie.

34

It took a week for Tweedle Dee and Tweedle Dum to fiddle around with mechanical devices and put the illusions together. Our job was to stay out of sight, which we did admirably.

At the end of the week, Tweedle Dee and Tweedle Dum outlined their plan. We met in the old gym building at our school. The school had built a new larger gym, with a full basketball court, and had stripped the old gym down to its wood floor and concrete walls in preparation for demolition. Fred explained that the half-court size of this old gym makes it the perfect place for the illusions they had in mind. Noises would be amplified nicely by the hard surfaces, the walls and floors, and images could be projected easily onto the bare walls. Ted said that it would be safe to use the place on a Saturday and Sunday because nobody would be around then.

"What about Lightning?" I asked. "He's always there."

"You mean, Max?" said Fred.

"Yeah."

"No problem," said Ted. "We worked out a deal with him. He won't be around."

Lightning was Max Frack, the old janitor guy. He practically lived at the school since his last wife died a year previously. He was a pleasant old duffer, with translucent skin and long white hair he wore in a pony tail long before there were hippies. He looked to be as old as Otto, but taller, willowy, and not quite as spry. All his movements, ambulation, speech, reactions, decisions, were tentative, slow to the point of madness if one was on a schedule. It was like watching a slow-motion movie. That's why we called him Lightning. Not to his face, of course.

Fred elaborated on their deal with Lightning. "For a bottle of Jack Daniels, he's gonna leave a bunch of extension cords lying around and just happen to be gone this weekend."

"Where'd you get the Jack Daniels?" I asked.

"Well … uhh … you see, since our mom went around the bend, our dad has been hittin' the booze pretty hard; so hard, in fact, that he don't keep count of the bottles. We took one of 'em. He'll never know the difference," they both said simultaneously.

They had opened a window to a subject I was curious about so I opened it a bit wider. "Does your mom ever come down?"

"Naw, we tried to talk to her but she doesn't answer questions. Sometimes she speaks, but it's in tongues so we have no idea what she's saying." Again they replied in unison, respect for the gravitas of the subject apparently causing this effect.

I wanted to press on but they did not appear eager to invite further questioning. The mood had become solemn. Nothing further was said for some long moments.

I looked over at Charlie and noticed he was looking at the ground, both eyes focusing on the same object. He appeared to be deep in thought, his face scrunched up as if he was trying to squeeze out words of consolation.

Burrupp! He squeezed out a fart.

Everyone laughed. The solemn mood was broken by comic relief, the drunk at the door.

Pudgy returned the discussion to details with a question about access to the old gym.

"No problem," said Fred. "We figured out how to pick the lock on the exit door long ago."

Ted chimed in—changing the subject slightly—explaining that timing and execution were the keys to their plan being successful. We would all have a role to play and we would have to practice until it was perfect. There would be visual effects, loud noises, screams, and surprises. The whole thing would have to happen within a few seconds in order for it to be frightening. The objective was to cause Socket Hair and his boys to associate the three of us with unimaginable terror, so they would be afraid to come near us, ever again. In other words, he said, "We hafta convince them that you guys are associated with magic, that it is unhealthy to mess with you."

"I like the unhealthy part," said Charlie.

"Good," said Fred, handing each of us a list of items to bring back next Saturday for the dress rehearsal. "The main event will be the next day, Sunday."

Charlie scratched his head, said to me and Pudgy, "Look what's on my list: an empty garbage can, a bullfrog, and two M-80 firecrackers."

"Lipstick, Brylcreem—ooh, A Little Dab'll Do Ya!—and black shoe polish on mine," said Pudgy.

"I got a bucket of old golf balls, and kite string," I said. "And I'm supposed to find out their real names."

"By the way," Ted said, "Our sister Janie, and her best friend Mary Lou, will be helping with this."

My eyes lit up.

"We need girls?" said Pudgy, unmoved as yet by the mysteries of the opposite sex.

"Certainly. They're gonna make the high-pitch screams ... unless you wanna do it," Ted said equably, as if explaining addition to a five-year-old.

"Oh, I get it," said Pudgy.

"Cool!" said Charlie.

I kept my mouth shut. Now that Pudgy and Charlie were fully on board with the plan, there was no need to oversell. When you win, don't appeal.

The whole deal was turning out as very good news from my point of view. It was distracting my friends from badgering me about the snake trick and it was giving me another opportunity to work my charms on Mary Lou. A twofer.

I thought that Charlie—ever optimistic, no matter the odds—might be indulging the same fantasy about Janie. I looked over at him, noticed the Mexican jumping bean, and hoped, for his sake, he could get the anticipation-jitters out of his system before she came in view of him again.

35

IT WAS MY TURN to prepare the message. The next Saturday, after the dress rehearsal, I went to Manny's Market and got another cardboard box. I scrawled the Wicca pentacle on two sides of the box as before. I put nothing on the other two sides. Inside the box, I placed a single piece of paper with a message. The message was written with individual letters cut out from a newspaper. It read:

"toMOrrow

oLd gyM

NOOn"

Then I slinked through the neighborhood, through backyards and over fences, to Socket Hair's house. I located his bike leaning on the front porch, waited until I was sure no one was looking, crept up, and placed the box next to the bike. As I was bending over, I noticed "Billy O'Reilly" written on the side of the bike. So that was his name. Then I ran like hell.

36

SUNDAY, NOON, WE WAITED inside the old gym. Tweedle Dee and Tweedle Dum were situated on a maintenance platform in the rafters above the center of the floor with a special slide projector they had made in the school shop. The projector was armed with two slides they had also made. One slide bore a crude image of Pudgy, the other a crude image of Charlie, both images taken at the dress rehearsal. The illusions.

Janie and Mary Lou were hidden behind the brothers' now-infamous electric chair, which had been appropriated for the event. It was placed against the far wall, directly opposite, and facing, the exit door. The brothers had modified the chair specially for this occasion. Loose wires and tree branches stuck out at odd angles from its arms and legs.

Charlie was in one corner of the far wall, hidden behind an empty garbage can. I was in the other far corner, opposite Charlie, behind a dark canvas I had borrowed from Otto when I went to the golf range to get the bucket of throw-away golf balls. Charlie and I bracketed the electric chair like parentheses.

Pudgy was standing in the exit doorway, waiting.

A minute after noon, Pudgy stepped inside the gym, raised two fingers in the air, nodded his head in a *yes* gesture, pulled the door behind him—leaving it open a crack—and retreated behind a pile of boxes left by workman in the near corner. Two fingers in the air was the signal that Billy O'Reilly was approaching with *two* confederates. The *yes* nod was the signal that the two were Iggy-Piggy.

We waited in silence.

The exit door squeaked open. A long sharp nose peeked in, sniffing the air like a mouse for cheese, followed by the face of its owner, Piggy. Before he could advance further, Socket Hair Billy wrestled him aside and looked in tentatively. Iggy stood behind Billy, looking over his shoulder. After a moment of uncertainty, as one, they stepped into the doorway and squinted at the electric chair at the opposite end of the gym. There were no windows in the gym and all the lights had been turned off. The only light came from the open exit door, which they were partially blocking. Their eyes had not yet adjusted to the darkness, so they were not sure what they were actually seeing.

The chair was sitting on a raised platform, looking more like a medieval throne than a chair, which was the point.

From behind, Janie shook the chair gently while Mary Lou manipulated thin stings attached to various branches. The branches swayed menacingly in the semi-darkness, as if the chair were alive, which was also the point.

Billy and Iggy-Piggy stepped into the gym and inched forward, straining to comprehend the scene. As they were moving, Pudgy, behind the boxes, was pulling on an unnoticed rope attached to the exit door, closing it gradually. By the time Billy and his pals realized the gym was darkening, they were midway across the floor, uncomfortably close to the chair. Iggy spun to look behind him at the door and caught a last look at daylight as Pudgy yanked the rope and the door slammed shut.

The gym plunged into total darkness.

Then all hell broke loose.

BLAM.

A brief flash and a deafening boom erupted from the garbage can in the far corner of the room, sounding like the 16-inch gun of a battleship.

Following immediately, a garbled female voice (Janie, through a cheerleader's megaphone muffled with a wad of newspaper) started keening, **"Great Motherrr Goddessss isss ... here ...,"** as a beam of light flashed briefly on a Wicca pentacle scrawled on the back rest of the electric chair.

Then blackness returned.

In the next instant, an image, covering the entire left side wall flashed for only a half-second, then another flashed on the right side wall, and the gym went dark again. The first image had been five times life-size: a giant beast that faintly resembled Pudgy. Black streaks ran down its face and enormous bare torso, black lips wore a hideous grimace revealing long, sharp incisors, and wild hair stood straight up. The second image was equally large and equally hideous, and faintly resembled Charlie. More black streaks, black raccoon eyes, and two horns. Gobs of a glistening substance drooled from its mouth. The images had flashed so fast that Billy and Iggy-Piggy only thought that's what they saw.

Two seconds later, a small beam of light from above clicked on a bullfrog hopping toward them from the garbage can corner. They stood fixed to the spot. One second, two seconds, three sec—**BLAM**—it disappeared, and a fine mist battered their faces.

Piggy screamed. Abject fear magnified the smell of him two-fold and filled the old gym with a noxious stench.

Iggy fell down, coughing.

Billy whimpered.

Another female voice crackled, **"Where … are you … Horned God?"** as I flipped a half-dozen golf balls into the air from my corner, causing random staccato sounds on the hardwood floor. At the same time, the twins flashed the images on the side walls again to reinforce whatever picture was in the heads of Billy and Iggy-Piggy.

Darkness again.

By now all three of them were whimpering, momentarily frozen in place like a dear in headlights, when a deep voice droned from above, **"Billy … this is … Horned God … the chair's for youuu.…"**

As this was being said, Mary Lou flipped a switch and the loose wires on the chair's arms and legs began to spark and crackle, punctuating the darkness, highlighting the waving branches, faintly illuminating the Wicca pentacle.

The image of Pudgy flashed one more time, one more fraction of a second, and bad-ass, boss-man, tough-guy, red-headed bully, Socket Hair Billy O'Reilly pissed his pants.

Iggy got up from the floor and started to drag Billy towards the exit door, at which time I pulled a string attached to a bucket in the rafters and a torrent of rock-hard golf balls rained down on them viciously.

Billy put his hands over his head like a toad in a hailstorm and found his own motivation for seeking the door. Piggy found him in the darkness and grabbed onto his shirt tail for guidance.

In blind panic, stumbling and falling on the golf balls, the three of them finally reached the exit door. Iggy fumbled to open it with Billy and Piggy fairly crawling up his back. **"Billy ... Billy ... Billlyyyy ...,"** wailed the Horned God from the bowels of the dark gym, as the door finally popped open and three scared rabbits sailed through it and disappeared into the neighborhood.

It took us less than four minutes to clear out of the old gym. Once we left, it was impossible to tell that anyone had been there. Charlie even cleaned up the frog splatter.

If Mrs. O'Reilly came to investigate the crime scene, she would discover nothing. If she interviewed any of the alleged perpetrators, she would discover dumb kids. We were good at dumb. She should understand that, since she had mothered the dumbest of the dumb.

As a social event, the two days were a bust. Mary Lou was her usual frosty self; she wouldn't give me the time of day. My best smile and consummate charm bought no moment with her. I thought this disingenuous, since she was wearing tight pedal-pusher pants again and was flashing her butt around with the obvious intention of distracting me from my assignments. She was one cool cookie. Sultry bitch.

Charlie fared no better. He couldn't get near Janie. She avoided him at every turn. When she heard that one of his assignments was his famous magic trick, she gagged. When he performed one at rehearsal, she barfed. Charlie couldn't win for losing.

Tweedle Dee and Tweedle Dum said not a word. They simply packed up and left, like gunfighters after the deed was done. They were cool.

We had new heroes.

37

BUT NOW I NEEDED ANOTHER DISTRACTION. I was pondering the dilemma behind my back porch where nobody could see me when Charlie saw me. I expected the usual harassment about pulling the snake gag when he surprised me with an idea he had for an entrepreneurial venture. He didn't quite put it that way; what he said was, "Hey, I got an idea how we can make a lotta money."

"I'm all ears," I said enthusiastically, hoping the idea would be brilliant and I could stretch it out for about thirty years. "What's the deal?"

"Gotta show ya, c'mon," he said, hurrying away.

Addressing his back, I said, "C'mon where?"

"The dump," he said, leading his sales pitch with a real hook. Without breaking stride, he called back, "You hafta see it with your own eyes, c'mon, let's go."

I ran after him.

"Whaddya talkin' about? See what?" I said.

"You'll see, just c'mon."

This seemed fair. Charlie had come along on several of my impromptu adventures purely on faith, so it was only fair that I do the same for him. I agreed, and we took off down the rutted dirt lane that led to the town dump.

The rutted dirt lane ran about two miles from the foot of our street to a main road connecting neighborhoods on the west side of town. It was a short cut, used rarely, and only on foot or bicycles. It was bordered on one side by the Woods, and on the other by a broad field of weeds and stubble, sometimes planted in cornflower, sometimes left fallow. The field was fallow now, burnt to a golden brown by the summer sun. About halfway down the lane, a wide footpath pierced the Woods and led to the rear of the town dump, our destination said Charlie.

Adjacent to the dump, a field of long narrow pits sat cooking in the sun. The pits had been gouged out by D-8 Caterpillar tractors into orderly rows, side-by-side like sergeant chevrons. The excavated soil was piled in orderly mounds between the pits. The pits were the final resting place of sludge removed from the bottom of septic tanks in the yards of homes not otherwise connected to a municipal sewer system. The septic tanks were cleaned out periodically by a commercial pumping service, the sludge vacuumed into tanker trucks and, in turn, emptied into the pits to dry. When the pits achieved a relative hardness, the D-8s covered them with the excavated soil. Over time, Mother Earth returned to her natural state. This was—and still is, in some rural areas—a common mode of public sanitation.

The pumping service was provided by a private company, owned by a colored-man, named William Johnson. The company was well-known in town—as one might expect—and operated its own fleet of trucks. There were some in town—the usual bigots—who considered that service an appropriate one for colored people. Bigots were few in number in Milford, and their ignorance caused them to miss the forest for the trees. William Johnson was a prominent citizen in the community. He brought his family to church on Sunday, just like everybody else. He bought groceries just like everybody else, and paid taxes just like everybody else. He was college-educated, soft-spoken, well-respected, and well-liked. He was a consummate businessman, and an "upper class" gentleman, if not *socially*, most certainly *financially*. He lived with his family quietly, in one of the best neighborhoods, in a fine home (served by a municipal sewer system) with an immaculately manicured lawn shaded by mature elms and maples. At the head of a long paved driveway, next to the mail box, he set a small traditional statue, the red-suited jockey tendering a brass ring. The jockey's face was painted white. William Johnson had class.

38

RATTLING DOWN THE LANE on my bike behind Charlie, I thought a little more about our destination. Of course, I had been forbidden to go to the dump, but like so many other forbidden places, I would go there anyway if I could fabricate—for my own self, that is—a rational exception to the rule. That's what I was doing now, fabricating. It wasn't so much disobedience as self-preservation. If I obeyed my mother literally, I would be thirty-five before I left my front yard.

I had been to the dump only once, with my dad, to unload some boxes of trash, and I really did not care for it. Flies, bugs and mice were everywhere. The smell was redolent of decay, decomposition, and methane. There were mountains and mountains of garbage, as far as the eye could see, or so it seemed, comprised of household objects not so much *used* as *dead*. Describing the place as depressing is putting a good face on it. Charlie, however, regarded the dump as a perfectly normal playground. To him it was his own personal amusement park. He frequented it regularly.

Charlie slowed his bike so I would catch up. As I came even with him, he continued his pitch on the attributes of the dump. "We're free there, man. We can throw rocks at birds and nobody cares. We can pee on bugs and mice. We can talk to the bums (he knew them by name). They're usually busy picking through the mounds of garbage, but I can get them to stop and tell dirty stories. They love to do that. You'll love Shorty, he's my favorite. He's only got one eye and no teeth, but he tells the funniest ones. I don't know where he lives. And, check this out, there's a calendar with a naked girl on it in the manager's shack, and you can see it if you stand on your tip-toes on a box and look through the window. Cool, huh? And when you get tired of that, we can go over to the pits and throw rocks into the soft ones. I like to get big rocks and pitch 'em like a shotput. It's pretty cool the way they plop and splash, like wet cement. You gotta stand back a bit or you'll get splashed with the stuff. That's the yucky part, so be careful."

He made the dump sound better than I remembered it. The "be careful" part at the end surprised me. So un-Charlie.

We stashed our bikes in some bushes just off the path and walked into the rear of the dump. First, Charlie said, we had to take a leak, then throw rocks at some birds, then go look at the naked girl. So we did. In that order.

It was a hot day, although not hot enough to broil the garbage and make the smell intolerable. A soft breeze helped. I was enjoying our little clandestine adventure, more than I had anticipated, and I was in no hurry to grill Charlie about his business idea. We looked for bums to chat with, but none were about, so we wandered over to the pits and started searching for rocks to shotput into the sludge. Almost immediately, I noticed there were tomato plants, laden with tomatoes, growing on the mounds of excavated soil between the pits. Tomatoes were everywhere, on all the mounds, and they were big, red, and beautiful.

I was stunned. I cried out, "Charlie, Charlie, look at this. There's tomatoes everywhere."

"No shit, Sherlock," he said, laughing heartily. "Took you long enough. This is what I wanted you to see. This is where I got the idea for *Charlie's Tomato Stand*."

"Say what?"

"We're gonna sell fresh tomatoes."

"*Charlie's Tomato Stand?*"

"Yup."

I was even more stunned. "You can eat these things?" I asked.

"Sure can. They're good," he said, biting into one and polishing another on his shirt for me. "Here, try one."

So I did. "Hmm, pretty good. Wait 'til Pudgy sees this."

Maybe Charlie wasn't so crazy after all, I thought. This might be a great idea.

But since it was to be our first business venture, I suggested to Charlie that we should get some adult advice. Charlie was skeptical at first, but finally agreed. It wasn't just *business* advice I was thinking about. I had an amorphous concern about the relationship between sludge and tomatoes.

The next day, Charlie and I went to consult the Oracle.

39

OTTO WAS FIDDLING with the ancient tractor as we approached. "Yo, Otto, howzit going?" I said, all smiles and charm.

"What is it now, fellas?" he said jovially, knowing we were up to something.

"We got this idea how to make a lotta money. It's Charlie's idea really, but it sounds pretty good to me."

"Let's hear it," he said.

Charlie told him.

He thought about it for a minute, then said, "No shit, Charlie, that's a great idea—whoa, I just made a pun."

"What's a *pun*?" Charlie and I said at the same time.

He looked at us like we were half-wits; then remembered we were only ten. Patiently, he said, "A pun is … uh … mixing of words in a funny way … like you just told me about sludge, and I said, 'No shit.' Get it?"

"Yeah, I guess so," I said.

Charlie looked confused, but kept quiet.

Otto continued, "Okay, back to the subject. I said the idea is a great one because what you just described is perfect organic gardening. Doesn't get any better'n that."

"What's *organic*?" Charlie asked.

"Means grown naturally, without fertilizer and shit—oops, I did it again."

"Did what?" I said.

"The pun, kid, the pun. I made another pun."

"Oh, I get it," I said, getting it this time.

Charlie nodded with a grin, suggesting he got it too.

"Good. So here's what you guys **hic** can do. Go get your other pal, the fat kid, Pudgy is it, cut him in on the deal, and the three of you go do it together. Whaddya waitin' for?"

Charlie and I looked at each other, absorbing the advice. Thinking.

Before we could answer, Otto continued, "You know, the money aside, it just might be a great gag. I mean, when people find out where the tomatoes come from, after they been gorging on 'em. Sure like to see the look on their faces. Oh well, don't worry about that. Just don't tell anyone I advised you to do it, okay?"

"Okay. Thanks Otto?" I said.

"Don't mention it."

"Why not?"

"That's just an expression. Means the same as *you're welcome*."

"Oh!"

40

CHARLIE AND I WENT HOME for lunch, agreeing to meet later that day in our conference room at the creek.

A couple hours later, when I finally wandered down there, I found Charlie sitting on a dry spot, serene, strangely contemplative, sporting a clean shirt and clean pants. I thought this quite odd. I thought I knew Charlie by now. I had never seen him in clean clothes, or sitting on a dry spot. The clean clothes, he explained, were required by his mother after he spilled a full bowl of pea soup on himself. I might have guessed the offending substance was pea soup, even if he hadn't told me, for the remains of it still on his shoes. And the flies. The dry spot was simply where one sat in clean clothes. I was perplexed by his strange serenity, until I noticed the bullfrog *ribbiting* some yards farther downstream and realized serenity was a state of mind that allowed both his eyes to focus on the same object at the same time. The contemplation, it became apparent, had to do with the bullfrog's future. I didn't want to dwell on how strange that might be; I wanted us to get down to business. But before we could do so, he rose and eased forward hypnotically to stalk the poor beast as if he had forgotten the purpose of our meeting.

"Hey, *Sherlock*, the tomatoes, remember?" I yelled.

He stopped in mid-stride, woke up it seemed, looked at me, "Oh yeah, okay, okay, the tomatoes." He said this absently; reluctant to see a fat juicy bullfrog hop away unmolested.

"Let's go find Pudgy then."

"Okay, let's go," he said cheerfully, as if I were the one obstructing progress.

We went over to Pudgy's house and I tapped on his bedroom window with a rake. Almost immediately, he came to the window, opened it, and asked what was going on.

Charlie explained his idea.

"I like it. Count me in," he said without hesitation, and climbed out of the window. "Let's go, let's go."

To this day, I wonder if hanging out with Charlie and me was harmful to Pudgy's childhood development or a contributing factor to his maturation. He had been sent to his room ten minutes earlier for a minor infraction of something. But now, presented with a new adventure, a new lease on life, he couldn't remember what the infraction was. *Here-and-Now* had more moment than *Wait-and-See*. He would embrace the new adventure and worry about climbing back through the window later. His mother would be none the wiser if he made it. So he'd chance it, as if his new motto had become: *If you don't ask, you can't get a no.* There was something symbolic in this. Pudgy was no longer a simple seeker of vicarious thrills. He had changed, gradually, and had become a principal player. The climb through the window was a symbolic passing, a completion of the transition. For good or bad.

As we bolted from the yard, Charlie said we should all be in the deal on equal terms, third-third-third, to which Pudgy and I readily agreed. Had Charlie been clever, he might have required a special percentage of the deal for his discovery of the tomatoes and rental of his front yard for retail sales. Sometimes, however, loyalty gained through equal partnership returns more dividends than cleverness. He didn't say that, but it was Wisdom-from-Charlie, nonetheless. Whaddya know?

By the end of the day, we had assembled boxes and baskets, and were prepared for the harvest.

Early the next day, we picked as many tomatoes as we could carry and hauled them to Charlie's house. At noon *Charlie's Tomato Stand* opened for business. We sold the smaller tomatoes for three cents and the larger ones for a nickel. We took turns working the stand and going door-to-door. When asked where the tomatoes were from, we fudged the answer by saying we had found a secret spot where a farmer's field spilled into some woods and nobody knew about it but us. The white lie lasted until Charlie's mother noticed we were generating an inordinate amount of income and demanded to know the truth.

Well, there's so much wool you can pull over a mother's eyes, so he had to tell her. She went nuts. I thought she was going to have a coronary. I thought his life was over when she said the dreaded words: "Wait 'til your father gets home."

He tried some really fast talking, spitting out the words without pausing for breath. "Ma, it's perfectly natural for seeds to pass through the human body and somehow end up on the ground and then plants spring up of their own free will because they wanna be born. That's nature's way. And look how beautiful these are. They're perfect. Here, taste one. They're from pure *organic* gardening. It don't matter that the seeds came from the sludge. Sludge ain't the same as shit—"

She slapped him. "Watch your language."

That was the end of our first entrepreneurial venture. A day and a half, and it was over. And we were turning a profit.

Oh well, I thought, look on the bright side; a *brief* distraction is better than *no* distraction at all. Kid Philosopher.

I was contemplating that last thought as I came in the back door of my house. My mother had just hung up the telephone.

"Just wait 'til your father gets home."

Oh shit! No pun intended.

41

THE FOLLOWING DAY, or the day after, or the day after that, Charlie and Pudgy were sure to come looking for me. No matter how hard I tried, and no matter what distraction I manufactured, they were sure to come prancing along, the two of them together, Frick and Frack, grinning like Cheshire cats, to bust my balls about avoiding the snake trick.

I knew if they cornered me I would have to go through with it. The best I could do was to make myself scarce.

Then I remembered the poodle Charlie was blamed for killing at the train station, and I thought, since that was pretty funny, I'd sneak off there and see what else was going on. There just might be some more laughs. I assumed I would not be identified as a co-conspirator in the murder, so I might be able to hang around for awhile unnoticed, and, more importantly, unfound.

I parked my bike against the side of the building and went in. Otto was behind the ticket window wearing the Station Master's hat.

"Yo, Otto, what're *you* doing here?" I said.

"Minding the **hic** store," he said.

"How come?"

"It's my day off. I'm minding things for my brother, Wendell. He hadda go to a dog funeral with Countess what's-her-name."

"Wendell's your brother?"

"Yeah."

"That mean your last name's Whippoorwill too?"

"Naw, he's my half brother."

"Oh!" I said, accepting the answer but not really understanding it. "So what's your last name then?"

"Oesterreicher."

"Ooo-ster-ryker?" I said, tentatively.

"That's close enough," he said. "Better'n most people, actually."

"What kinda name is that? Polish or something?"

"Austrian."

What's that?"

"The language of the country called Austria."

"Where they have kangaroos?"

"No, that's *Australia*, with an 'al.' There's no kangaroos in *Austria*,"

"Oh!"

Apparently Otto was feeling effusive today, so he added, "Austria is a country in Europe. My father grew up there, in a city called Vienna. My mother grew up in Hungary, the country next door. When they got married, Austria and Hungary were feuding, preparing to go to war with each other. That made things pretty messy for them, so they moved to America."

"Oh, so then, you're an Austrian?"

"No. I was born here, after my parents arrived. That makes me an American. Just like you. Wendell too."

"Oh!"

"Got it now?" he said, mirthfully.

"Yeah, I think so. But *Oos-ster-whatsis* is a mouthful. Maybe I should call you *Double-O*, or how 'bout *Oh-Oh*?" I joked.

"That's okay, *Francis*." Comedian.

I thought it was a good time to stop trying to be cute, so I asked respectfully, "Why's Wendell care about a dog funeral?"

"He don't. He just went **hic** cuz he's hot for the Countess."

"Yuck!"

Then she walked in the door, on the arm of Wendell P. Whippoorwill. She was wrapped in numerous layers of black gauze—mourning attire, presumably—that floated about her immense frame like parachute silk in a light breeze. Her eyes were red and swollen from sobbing. Her face was lined with mascara and sorrow.

Wendell was oblivious, enjoying the progress of his amorous intentions even if their first date had to be a dog funeral. He was beaming from ear to ear as if he was escorting Miss America. The picture was as cute as it was comical.

If the Countess was aware of Wendell's effulgence, she was not amused. The funeral had merely exacerbated a disposition which had been sour since the day her poodle met the train. Her expression had been rather abstract until she saw me. As if awakened from a deep sleep, her eyes popped wide; she pointed a fat finger at me, and cried, **"Hey, that's the friend of that filthy little urchin that killed my Horseshit."**

"What'd ya say?" asked Wendell P.

"I said, that's the—"

"Hold on, wait a minute," interrupted Otto. "Don't be hollerin' at the kid. He ain't done nothing."

"—well … well … I … I …," she sputtered, clearly lathering up for something. And whatever it was, judging from her tone and volume, it could not be good.

I quickly concluded that Otto's comments on my behalf were all that needed to be said on the subject, and that I should anoint my conclusion with immediate departure.

"Later, Otto," I said, and ran like hell. It seemed I was doing a lot of that lately.

42

THE NEXT DAY, I went to Lacey's Golf Range to thank Otto for coming to my assistance at the train station. He was still fussing with the engine of the ancient tractor.

"Damn thing won't start," he said, banging on the carburetor with a wrench.

"That oughta fix it," I said, thinking I was a great wit.

"Don't be **hic** a smart ass. Whaddya want?" he said gruffly, irritated at the tractor, not at me.

"Sorry. Just wanna thank you for helping me out yesterday, that's all."

"Don't mention it."

"Why not?" I said, with a straight face.

"It's just an expression—whoa … sonofabitch … you got me. You are a smart ass," he said, with a sincere belly laugh, happy to return to his cheerful self.

"Couldn't help myself," I said. "Anyway, thanks again. I'll see ya later."

"Wait a minute," he said, grinning from ear to ear. "How's the tomato business?"

I told him.

This time he laughed so hard, tears ran down his cheeks. "Don't blame me."

"Ain't your fault," I said.

"Good. Then thanks."

"Don't mention it," I said this time.

We both laughed at that; then he said, "So, if you're out of a job, maybe I got something for you here. You wanna work on Saturday?"

"Doin' what?"

"Picking up golf balls. I'm not gonna have this tractor working for another few days, and I'm running out of balls here. I need someone to go out on the driving range and pick up balls."

"Wearing a coat of armor?"

"Very funny."

"Sorry," I said.

"Okay, here's the deal. We don't open 'til 10:00 AM, so you can start at 8:00 or 9:00, or whenever you want. You just pick up as many balls as you can until 10:00. Penny a ball."

"That's all we gotta do?" I said, thinking this would be like found money. Honest money too, that I wouldn't get in trouble for.

"Yeah, that's all. And there are plenty of balls out there **hic,** so you can bring Charlie and Pudgy if they wanna work too."

"Perfect," I said, already thinking how to turn this into another reprieve. "I'll see ya Saturday."

I found them down at the creek. Charlie was fiddling with some matches and cardboard, about start a fire. There were no frogs or tadpoles or other living creatures in sight, so Pudgy was wondering what Charlie was up to this time.

"Hey, you guys wanna make some money?" I said, before they could get their mind on the snake trick.

"How?" they said at the same time, a little gun-shy after the tomato deal.

I told them the new deal.

"It'll be easy, like pickin' cotton," I said. "We'll each have a bag or a can or something, and all we hafta do is pick up as many golf balls as we can, and we get a penny for each one."

"Cool!" said Pudgy, his mind already tasting the cakes and sweets the money would buy.

"Okay!" said Charlie, not wanting to be left out.

We showed up at Lacey's Golf Range a little before 9:00 on Saturday morning. Otto handed us some bags and buckets, and pointed to the driving range.

"You'll probably find most of the balls between the "50 Yards" sign and the "150 Yards" sign," he said. "But don't look just there. The total area is about ten acres, and I ain't been out there with the tractor for a **hic** couple days, so there's balls everywhere."

Ten acres did not register with me yet.

So out we went, with our bags and buckets, visions of entrepreneurial wealth dancing in our heads, into a morning sun delighted to start its workday beaming UV rays on three new targets that hadn't thought to wear hats and would soon shed their shirts.

Golf balls were not stacked three-deep, waiting for easy pick up. On the contrary, balls were spaced yards apart, sometimes many yards apart, and were spread randomly over the entire driving range. Ten acres.

At first we hustled from ball to ball, running sometimes, quick-walking sometimes, seeing pennies not balls, showing greed not industry. The sun was grateful for our company, and sent its thanks in ever increasing intensity. Gradually, we slowed down and found a tolerable working pace.

Just as we settled into a rhythm, two smudges eased into my peripheral vision, far to the left, moving slowly in our direction. It was not uncommon for folks to cut across the driving range, taking their chances when the range was open and balls were whizzing by, so I paid little attention to this movement. When it became apparent that the two smudges were kids about our size, I began to take notice. I was, however, still greedily engrossed in snatching golf balls, and gave no further thought to the matter, even when I heard something plop on the ground ten yards away. Then something plopped near Charlie, and I looked over to see a golf ball bounce and roll. Charlie looked up quizzically. "What's going on?" he said. "The driving range ain't supposed to be open yet."

When I returned to regard the smudges, they had come closer and resolved themselves into Iggy Plicket and something else further back, and they were throwing golf balls at us. The smudges kept advancing and the something else resolved itself into two figures, the foremost of which was the midget Piggy, barely indistinguishable from the background figure, who else but Socket Hair too-dumb-to-quit-trying Billy O'Reilly. Billy's arm was cocked and he was preparing to fire another golf ball. This was a planned attack. We were at it again.

Apparently, we were not as clever as we thought we were. They never saw us that day at the old gym, which they had fled quicker than pigs from a gun, yet somehow they credited us with perpetrating the event. How did they figure that out, I wondered?

Ordinarily, when confronted by these buffoons, we would turn tail and depart the scene at full speed. Abundance of caution was our ordinary motto; a good one to live by, in a world of Billy O'Reillys and Iggy-Piggies. But this scene was not ordinary, for a very good reason—they were attacking *guns* in a field of *bullets*. They just didn't know that yet.

Charlie and I were addicted to balls. To be more precise, we were addicted to the throwing of balls. In fact we were addicted to the throwing of anything. Baseballs, softballs, whiffle balls, footballs, tennis balls, basketballs, dirtballs, snowballs, darts, sticks, and stones (Charlie had even thrown Jello). When there was no game in which to throw a ball, we threw balls to each other. When we were alone, we threw things at targets drawn on walls or cans placed on a post. At Scripps Pond, we skipped flat stones across its surface and threw round ones at frogs. Sometimes, we just went into Charlie's back yard and threw rocks at birds and trees. We threw darts in my basement, and broomsticks in the yard. We threw chalk in the classroom, and dirtballs in the schoolyard. We threw cornflower stalks and acorn squash at harvest time. We threw snowballs in the winter. We had become quite proficient.

Pudgy was not quite as fanatical about throwing things as Charlie and I were, but he hung around with us enough to get in more than the average kid's ration of throwing. In spite of himself, he had a damn fine arm. Charlie and I, on the other hand, had *guns*.

So, into this context waltzes Iggy-Piggy and Socket Hair Billy, approaching from the east, picking up golf balls as they advanced and throwing them at us.

43

"LOOK AT THIS WILL YA?" I said to Charlie. "Are they doin' what I think they're doin'?"

"Looks like!"

"They're attacking us with golf balls?"

"Looks like," he said, again.

"I don't believe it."

"You better, there's a ball headin' your way right now. Watch out!"

"Oh man!" I said. "Will they ever learn? And look at Piggy. What's that he's doing?"

"He's throwing like a girl," Charlie said, matter of factly. "You never seen that before?"

"No!"

"Well take a good look then, because it's quite rare."

And it was. I was astounded. I had never seen a boy throw like a girl. I couldn't imagine such a thing, but there it was. "Jeez! That's pitiful."

"Whoopee!" said Charlie quietly, before cupping his hands to his mouth and bellowing at Piggy, **"Sisseeee."**

I felt bad for Piggy. I disliked him intensely, but I still felt bad for him. Throwing like a girl. How tragic to be defective so early in life. Had he no shame?

There is no excuse for a boy throwing like a girl. Boys just *do not* throw like girls. Men especially do not throw like girls. They just don't. *That* is an immutable law of nature. It is not just common knowledge. It is Written. Everywhere. In the *Epic of Gilgamesh*. In the *Rosetta Stone*. In the *Upanishads*.

"The Man Shalt Not Throw Like A Girl," was intended to be the Eleventh Commandment (and would have been had not the third tablet been dropped by Moses and shattered and lost forever, according to an historical documentary by Mel Brooks, *The History of the World, Part One*).

Call it the *act* of throwing, the *art* of throwing, the *skill* of throwing, they are all the same. The importance of this issue cannot be over-stated. It is neither irrelevant nor innocuous.

The proper throwing of projectile weapons by the unaided arm of Man is pertinent to the evolution not just of sports but to all of civilization. It has played an unheralded role in sorting species, forging reputations, and shaping nations. Homo sapiens would not have overpowered the Neanderthals throwing stones like a girl. The Three-hundred Spartans did not hold off Xerxes's vaunted army throwing spears like a girl. Alexander did not become *The Great* rampaging through Asia Minor with his Macedonians hurling missiles like queens. Spartacus's warriors did not throw like girls, nor did Shaka Zulu's, or Braveheart's. The list goes on and on.

Particularly poignant is a haiku, attributed to an anonymous seventeenth-century samurai, who theorized that the only way to defeat the famous swordsman, Miyamoto Mushashi, was by standing off several sword-lengths and hurling something at him. Ironically, this haiku is particularly applicable to the present-day use of the hand grenade:

Throw like girl
Die quick

History shows plainly that boys throw like boys *naturally*. Boys learn to throw things coincident with taking their first steps, sometimes before. Sure, girls can throw like boys, but they're not born with the ability, they have to learn it. And many do, to their great credit. But boys are born with it. What happened to Piggy?

Then I thought, "Why should I feel bad for him? After all, I wasn't attacking *him*, he was attacking *me*. Shouldn't this be his problem?"

Poor slob. If he didn't learn to throw properly, the stigma of throwing like a girl would dog him in adulthood worse than a heart-shaped tattoo of a lost lover. How could he play touch football at a Labor Day picnic? How could he play softball for the office team? What would he teach his kids? A dart game in a biker bar would be fun to watch.

I was still reflecting on Piggy's manhood when a ball thrown by Iggy plopped on the ground close by. I came back to my senses and noticed that Billy was fixing to fire one too. My sympathy for Piggy evaporated.

"Hey Bucky Beaver," I yelled at him. "Your sister teach you to throw like that?"

By way of an answer, his face reddened with anger. He fumed. Then—picture this—his right elbow came up and pointed at me, his upper arm remained parallel to the ground, and his fist pulled back cradling a golf ball. He stood like a ballerina, a grim determination furrowing his brow.

What is he doing?

Then, without the slightest movement of his torso or upper arm, he snapped his ball hand forward like a catapult, flicked his wrist like a maypole dancer, and unleashed the ball in my direction. A *take-that-you-beast* expression of satisfaction emasculated his face.

The ball arced like a rainbow, sailed at least fifteen feet, bounced along the ground another fifteen feet, and dribbled to a stop twenty feet from my shoes.

He was impervious to shame.

Even Pudgy, ever so effeminate—owing mostly to shiny clothes and slicked-down hair—did not throw like a girl.

44

WE COULD NOT POSSIBLY run from this situation. It was too good. So we stood our ground. Guns in a field of bullets.

They spread out, three abreast, advanced slowly to within about twenty yards and stopped, facing us. We were still well out of Piggy's range, but that didn't seem to occur to Captain Billy.

We faced them. The Ball Fight at the OK Corral.

A soft wind kicked up tiny dust devils, ruffled Pudgy's hair, and whisked the smell of Piggy away from us.

Birds chirped, a dog barked, and the white noise of a Saturday morning purred softly—while I affected boredom.

Flies buzzed lazily around Charlie's shoes. His focus was so intense that his game eye settled into perfect alignment with his good eye and together they shot laser beams at the enemy.

The low, morning sun shone brightly behind us, casting long shadows on the ground, and blinding light into the enemies' eyes.

They stood motionless, squinting.

We stood motionless, waiting.

The air crackled with tension.

Ike Clanton drew first. He fired at Pudgy, hitting him in a soft spot on his right side, soiling his clean shirt, causing no damage otherwise. Pudgy was infuriated, his outfit tarnished. He smiled menacingly as his throwing arm swelled like Popeye's after a can of spinach.

Billy Clanton drew next, fired at Charlie, grazing his left (non-shooting) arm. Charlie smirked, and silently brushed flies off his shoes, the gesture dripping with disdain.

Frank McLaury fired at me, missing widely.

I feigned a smile, as absent of mirth as if I'd swallowed a fly.
A long second went by.
I looked to my right, "Ready, Virgil?"
"Yep!"
I looked to my left, "Ready, Doc?"
"Ready, Wyatt."
Another long second went by.
"Fire boys," I said.

We let loose a withering barrage, throwing as fast as we could pull balls from our bags. Our arms worked like automatic weapons, spraying them while they bent for balls on the ground, just rewards for not having the foresight to load pockets with balls or carry them in a bag. Recompense for their tactical error.

Iggy's red and green elf outfit was a colorful attraction, in the convenient way of the British redcoat. He tried to smile and his too-white teeth flashed like a beacon in the morning sun, screaming *target, target*, redundantly. He took a few well-earned hits from all of us but didn't back down until Charlie hit him with a glancing blow on the top of his head. He cried out in pain, startling his mates. He stood still for a moment, momentarily dazed. He reached up, felt his head, and when his hand came down with a speck of blood on it he went pale. Slowly, he started drifting backwards, terrified and effectively out of action.

Piggy yelped and hobbled backwards from a blow to his right leg, and one to his stomach. His throwing arm was pathetic; he might as well have been throwing daisies. Tears formed in his eyes. When he saw Iggy drifting away, his enthusiasm for the fight evaporated. He covered his head with his hands and limped away in fright.

Our firing continued, unrelenting, intense, and overpowering.

As Iggy-Piggy withdrew, Billy became the prime target. We honored the distinction with a rain of balls. He brushed off several hits to the body, arms and legs; and when one nearly took off an ear, he reluctantly back-pedaled. When he saw that his army had collapsed behind him, he withdrew in earnest.

Then they were in full retreat, running scared. We chased them a few yards for show, continuing to fire until they were out of range and gone.

It was another humiliating defeat for Billy O'Reilly, one that begged the question: was he really that stupid? Performance speaks for itself. He had led a discretionary attack, against a superior force, *into* the sun, without a plan, without adequate ammunition, with fully one-third of his force incapable of meaningful participation. Amazing! This was ignorance of astounding proportions, ignorance that earns a student a failing grade, a soldier a bullet, a general a defeat, and a president a doomed republic. The good news for the republic is that Billy was destined to spend a lifetime toiling for a passing grade.

We were rejoicing our victory when we looked down at our bags and realized we had shot off almost all our balls. The demands of combat, overwhelming and unavoidable, had depleted our fortunes. Such is war.

It was now 9:45. We had fifteen minutes to replenish our supplies. We resumed the earlier mad dash to collect balls. A minute before 10:00, huffing, puffing, and sweating, we shuffled into the ball shack, where Otto sat grinning, enjoying an ice cold Nehi.

"Who won?" he said, looking at me.

"We did ... I guess."

"You bring any balls back?"

"Some."

"Youse wanna **hic** work again tomorrow?"

"Don't think so."

We counted out our balls. Charlie had 194, I had 192, and Pudgy 213.

Otto was happy to get the additional balls, even though he had expected more and would have had a lot more but for our little war. He was generous, nonetheless; he gave me and Charlie two bucks each, and Pudgy two and a quarter. He also gave each of us a free Nehi. That made the day.

Although each of us had a few bruises, none were serious and none caused any visible damage or limping. I made up another little white lie that I had to go with my family to visit my grandmother on Sunday as an excuse to decline Otto's offer to work that day. Charlie and Pudgy bought it too, so we declared Sunday a day of rest. We were, under the circumstances, content with our earnings. It was not the most money we had ever held in our hands, but it belonged to us fair and square, and nobody else. And we wouldn't be in trouble this time, assuming, that is, that none of our adversaries expired on their way home.

It was a good day when we weren't in trouble for something.

45

THE NEXT DAY I went over to Charlie's house intending to distract him once again by suggesting an adventure to Manny's Market to spend our money.

As I walked down the street, I noticed a yellow taxi sitting by the curb in front of Charlie's house. The taxi's engine was turned off and its driver was seated at the steering wheel reading a newspaper. I paid this no mind.

When I knocked on the front door, Charlie's mother answered and invited me in. The Miller house had no vestibule or foyer, so the front door led immediately into the left-hand corner of the living room.

I walked in.

The living room was small, the same as mine, and the same as all the other living rooms in all the other cookie-cutter homes in our neighborhood, all built from the same set of architectural plans.

A flower-print sofa against the opposite wall faced the front door, its position the most logical for the room and virtually the same as every other sofa in every other home in the neighborhood.

Facing the sofa, and to my right, were two large arm-chairs, generously upholstered in hues and patterns compatible with those of the sofa. In the center of this arrangement was a rectangular coffee table, upon which was set a marble ashtray, a silver box with wooden matches, and small crystal duck.

The room was tidy, pleasantly utilitarian, and reflected pride of ownership.

Charlie was seated on the edge of the far-most arm-chair staring at the duck. If he appeared to be deep in contemplation, it would be incorrect to assume he was regarding the duck. He was, in fact, regarding the matches and how he might gain some when the coming charade was over.

Facing Charlie, and occupying a large portion of the sofa, was the Countess Abigail Fensterwald, the apparent passenger of the waiting taxi. She had called upon the Miller household unannounced, a scant two minutes before my arrival. She was swathed in her usual multi-layered ensemble. On this occasion, a sturdy beige fabric was wrapped around her horizontally giving the unsettling impression she'd been rolled in it like a burrito. No breeze was about to flutter the fabric and soften the look. The odd fashion was complemented by an expression of sullen arrogance. She sat inert, as if The Mountain should have come to her.

I started to back out the door when Charlie's mother said the last thing I wanted to hear: "Why don't you have a seat there next to Charlie?" The question was delivered politely, with a tinge of motherly authority, so I nodded agreement.

I wandered over and plunked down next to Charlie, who looked like he'd rather be dipped in hot oil than seated across from the burrito.

Charlie's mother sat down in the near-most arm-chair, brushed back an errant strand of hair, and said, "Now what is it that brings you here Mrs. Fensterwald?"

The use of *Mrs.* was intentional. Small town gossip had gotten around even to our neighborhood, and Charlie's mother had heard the stories of Abigail Fensterwald's instant Countess-ship. The *instant* aspect of the title the Countess affected was not responsible for the dubious reputation that preceded her. Most people in town were sympathetic to the sudden loss of her husband on their wedding day. And some even respected her for choosing to settle in the same town. She had, however, managed to burn off most of the sympathy and respect by an ostentatious display of wealth and superiority, flaunting her jewelry around town and disdaining friendly discourse. Charlie's mother was neither impressed nor amused by the Countess. Her arrival by taxi—unannounced and untimely—did not set the stage for a pleasant interview.

Sadly, Abigail Fensterwald of Cuyahoga Falls, Ohio was not smart enough to let the *Mrs.* pass. Instead she said, "*Countess* Fensterwald, if you please, Mrs. Miller."

"Certainly," said Charlie's mother equably. Her tone was vastly more polite than the correction and was followed by a noticeably terse, "What brings you here?"

The Countess was not entirely uncivil. She was aware that the decibel level of speech she usually employed was unsuitable for the small room in which she now sat, and equally unsuitable for the purpose of her visit. She said quietly, "That boy killed my dog."

"By 'that boy,' are you referring to my Charles?"

"Yes, the scruffy one sitting there," she said, pointing to Charlie.

Charlie's mother turned beet-red and steam seemed to leak from her ears, but she bit her lip and remained composed. She straightened her skirts and asked, "And how exactly did he do that?"

"He chased my poor little Horseshit out of the train station, onto the platform, and into an on-coming train."

"I beg your pardon?"

"What?" blurted the Countess.

"What is that language you are using in my home? You said he chased *what?*"

"Horseshit," the Countess answered, dragging the *oar* and emphasizing the *shhicked*. "That is the name of the dog, after the given name of my departed husband, Count Orschicht Fensterwald of Bavaria."

"I see," said Charlie's mother icily, disliking this phony Countess and recognizing the need to affect an attitude of her own. "Is that true Charles?"

Charlie fidgeted for a moment, caught unawares. He had been enjoying the spectacle of someone other than himself brought up short by his mother for use of foul language. Finally he blubbered,

"No Ma, honest! I wasn't chasing the dog, I was just trying to catch it. I was trying to help."

Then she looked at me. "Were you there, Sonny Boy? Did you see what happened?"

I had been following the exchanges with more than idle curiosity, so I was ready with my reply. "Yes ma'am, I was there. It was just as Charlie said."

"Well, of course he'd agree. They're birds of a feather, them two," the Countess charged, in perfect Cuyahoga Falls-ese.

At this point, Charlie's mother ran out of patience, but not out of composure. She decided to take control of the discussion with a view of ending it. Politely, she addressed the Countess, "We seem to have a difference of opinion here, which brings us back to my original question of why you are here. Were you expecting we would conclude that Charles did in fact kill your dog and that he should be punished somehow?"

"No! Not mere punishment, Mrs. Miller. I should think some form of recompense would be in order," replied the Countess, employing language and sentence structure obviously memorized for this occasion and clearly beyond that learned in Cuyahoga Falls.

"Recompense? Recompense?" Charlie's mother said softly, almost to herself.

"Yes. For my loss," the Countess said when she should have shut up.

Charlie's mother lowered her head imperceptibly, appeared to be thoughtful, and let the words sink in. A few awkward moments passed in which it may have appeared she did not understand the term *recompense*, when in fact she was merely controlling her rage and preparing an appropriate response.

Then she stood and fixed Abigail Fensterwald with a blistering gaze that should have sent her scurrying. When it didn't, she said sternly, "Your *loss*? Your *loss*? The only thing you seem to have *lost* is your wits."

"You can't talk to me—"

"*I am not done*, madam," interrupted Charlie's mother, on a roll now. "You see my sleeves rolled up? That's for mopping the floor, surely not for fashion. See these hands? See how red they are? That's from doing laundry. I just washed a load, and Charles helped me put it through the ringer. I was about to go out in the yard and hang it on the line when you knocked on my door. Your timing was inconvenient, but I invited you in nevertheless. Then you proceeded to insult my son, and to insult me as well. You talked down to me as if you're a real countess and I'm a commoner. Well, *Mrs.* Fensterwald, here's the way it is. We are a working-class family. We have no money for shopping in New York. No money for the kind of jewelry you so shamelessly display. And *certainly*, no money for **recompense**."

Again, the Countess should have left it at that and gracefully departed. Instead, she tried one more time. "Fair is fair. He killed my dog and I should be entitled to compensation."

That did it.

"**Out! Out!**" screamed Charlie's mother, as she held the door open with one hand and motioned the Countess through it with the other.

Countess Abigail Fensterwald flinched in surprise. She hefted her bulk from the sofa, pointed her nose in the air, feigned indignation, and flowed out the door like a slow tide, leaving *humph* and *well-I-never* sounds in her wake.

The yellow taxi sped from the curb, the taxi driver unaware he was about to be anesthetized by a random account of death and injustice.

"*Charles?*" I said to Charlie later.

"What'd you expect, *Howdy Doody?*"

We were sitting on the grass in Charlie's backyard next to the fence where Old Man Kramer had nailed back the slats covering our secret hole. We were having a great yuck over his mother's thrashing of the stupid Countess and looking wistfully at our lost shortcut.

"How many times has he nailed the slats back," I asked Charlie.

"Three, I think."

"We can pry 'em off again, but sooner or later he's gonna get tired of that and tell our parents," I said.

"Yeah, maybe we should cool it for awhile. If we wait a bit, he might forget about it and stop checking. Old people forget stuff quickly, ya know."

"Maybe we could fix up some kinda hinges so the slats would look closed but we could open 'em like a door when we need to."

We were contemplating this strategy when Charlie's dad, home from work, pulled his 1949 Ford into the driveway and got out with a six-pack of beer in his hand. He waved cheerfully to us and went in the back door to the kitchen.

Charlie lit up with a grin and said, "Let's go listen by the kitchen window. Maybe we can hear what my mom says about the fat lady."

There was an old wooden crate under the back porch and Charlie pulled it around under the kitchen window. The day was warm and the window was open. The screen was in place to keep out insects, but would not degrade the sound of people inside talking.

We balanced ourselves on the crate and listened as Charlie's mother related the story.

When she finished, his dad laughed hysterically. "Good job, honey," he said. Then he sat down at the kitchen table, opened a can of beer with a metal can opener, took a sip, and mumbled, "Countess, my ass."

For the first time all day, Charlie's mother smiled.

46

I MANAGED TO AVOID Pudgy and Charlie for the rest of that week. Apparently I had gotten so good at it they were not even aware I was intentionally avoiding them. The problem was: I was running out of places to hide.

The next weekend I *actually* had to go out of town with the family to visit relatives. That took care of another Saturday and Sunday. On Monday, I slipped away on my bike and headed over to see Otto at Lacey's Golf Range.

"Yo, Otto, howzit goin'?," I said, with my widest smile and friendliest voice. I wasn't concerned about wearing out my welcome, I was only ten.

"You again?" he said.

"Those bullies are looking for trouble again," I said.

"Is that a surprise?" he said, rhetorically.

"Well, I was hoping they would get the message and leave us alone."

"Why should they? Remember, I told you it wouldn't be a good idea to 'engage them directly?' Don't go at 'em directly, I said. Remember that?" he said, rather gruffly.

"Yeah, I remember."

"And what did you do? You messed with 'em head on at the old gym, and then again last week, right here at the driving range," he said, a little less gruffly.

"I thought we were cool at the old gym. We stayed hidden. They never saw us. Then, out here last week, they came right at us. We had no choice. Besides, we knew we had the advantage. We just couldn't help ourselves. It was like shooting fish in a barrel," I said defensively.

"Excuses, excuses, excuses," he said. "You just keep provoking them, and they keeping coming after you, and you wonder why. Nothing changes. You guys don't seem to learn."

"*Prohking* them? What's that mean?"

"Not *prohking*, it's *pro-voking*. There's a 'V' in the middle," he said, patiently.

What's *provoking* mean?"

"Means … like teasing, getting them mad at you."

"They're already mad at us."

"You're missing the point. Let's not debate it," he said.

"What's *debate* mean?"

"Means … argue."

"Who's arguing?"

"Aaahh! … kid, yer killin' me."

"I wouldn't kill you."

At this, Otto burst into a fit of laughing. A conversation with a ten-year-old can drive a person to distraction if he doesn't find the humor in it. And the patience. He wiped a tear from his eye, gathered his composure, and said, "You know what I mean."

"Yeah, you're right. I guess we messed up, huh?"

"Bingo," he said, softly, but not unkindly. If he was a bit frustrated with our conversation he didn't show it.

Therein transpired another of Otto's interminable periods of silence, to which I had become accustomed, but still found unsettling. I had learned, however, that if I did not press a point immediately, Otto would eventually return to it, most likely in a better mood.

I busied myself for about fifteen minutes, rearranging buckets of golf balls, straightening up the golf club rack, then headed over to the counter to assess Otto's mood. A couple of customers arrived just at that point, so I did an about-face and stayed out of sight until they left. Kids were tolerated around the driving range, but were not to be seen or heard when customers were present. We could never wear out our personal welcome with Otto, such was his nature, but we could easily get kicked out of the place by David B Lacey's father, who was, after all, running a business not a nursery school.

Eventually the customers left and I was able to amble back over to Otto. He looked at me, faking a straight face, unable to hide the mirth sparkling in his deep-set eyes. "So what is it now?" he said. This was the good Otto, the one I needed. My patience was rewarded.

"Pudgy got a note from that red-headed kid, Billy O'Reilly. He's the boss of them three. He wants to meet us at Silver Beach to settle things once and for all. I don't really know what that means, but it can't be good," I said.

"You're right for once **hic,** Sonny Boy."

"Okay, lemme think. They're already *provoked*, so it's too late do anything about that. And … the other thing we shouldn't do is *engage* 'em, right?" I said, proudly employing the new word.

"Bingo again, Sonny Boy."

Then he went quiet again, which was okay this time because I had just scored two *rights* and I knew something was developing. So I waited … and waited.

When I couldn't stand it any longer, I said, "So, whaddya think?"

"Nothin'," he said. "I don't think nothin'."

"Oh."

"What I mean is: you got the answer already. You just said it yourself, shouldn't *engage* 'em. Ain't that what you just said?"

"Well, yeah, but … then what?" I said.

"Remember me?" he said. "I'm just the idea man. I gave you the idea, long time ago. You already know all you need to know to deal with the situation yourself. You guys just hafta figger out the **hic** details yourself, that's all."

"Okay … okay," I said, half-heartedly, knowing that was all I would get from Otto. He was right as usual. The rest was up to us.

47

"OKAY, PUT OUT THE FIRE," I said to Charlie the next day at the creek. "We gotta figure this out."

Pudgy was already there, bent over, adjusting some kindling wood in the fire for Charlie, who was trying to wave me off, clearly not wanting an interruption.

"Awhhh, not now," complained Charlie. "I got some tadpoles here, coupla fat ones, just beggin' to be popped." If nothing else, Charlie was consistent.

"Later with that! Those bullies sent Pudgy a note. They wanna fight us to the finish," I said, trying to make it sound serious enough to divert Charlie's attention away from tadpoles begging to be sacrificed to whatever deities danced in his mind. "We gotta figure somethin' out or they're never gonna let us alone."

"All right, all right," Charlie said, with a loud authoritative voice I had not heard before, pouring the tadpoles out in the creek. "Be free, be free, little tadpoles."

I thought I was hallucinating.

The note to Pudgy dared us to meet them at *Silver* Beach at *noon* the next day. We discussed various strategies, and decided we would accept the dare, but on our terms, not theirs. We needed to control the outcome.

We sent a note back to them saying we would be at *Gulf* Beach at *4:00 PM* the next day.

48

THE PLEASANT NEW ENGLAND TOWN, Milford, Connecticut, enjoys seventeen miles of shoreline on Long Island Sound, a body of water stretching from New York City to Rhode Island. The dictionary says a *sound* is a narrow passage of water. But along the south-facing Connecticut coast, Long Island Sound is so wide that Long Island is a thin line on the horizon, visible only on the clearest of days. On the clearest of nights, lights can just barely be seen, twinkling faintly. In winter, snow flurries and icy gale-force winds invest Long Island Sound with an ocean-like status; in summer, sailboats and sport fisherman do the same.

Most of the town's shoreline is sandy beach, punctuated by occasional rock outcroppings, a few stone walls, and the entrance to the town's only harbor. Virtually all stretches of sandy beach not designated public beach park are lined with vacation cottages owned and occupied by wealthy New Yorkers whose visits were limited to the summer months.

The approach to the town's harbor is a wide mouth, funnel-shaped, flanked on the east by a popular public beach, known as Gulf Beach, and on the west by a long rock jetty. The harbor is gained through a short narrow channel—the spout of the funnel—less than a quarter mile in length. Once through the channel, the waterscape opens abruptly, generously, into a typical, picturesque New England harbor. A mile inland, the harbor narrows, and peters out in the center of town, alongside the dusty field where sits Bushnell's Turtle.

By city standards, the harbor is small. It is not a deep-water port and does not accommodate container ships and ocean-liners. Most every useful square foot of the harbor is taken up with docks, piers, private pleasure craft, a yacht club, and a small commercial fishing and oyster harvesting operation. The tableau—of sailboats and motorboats bobbing lazily in their berths while others maneuver carefully about in the requisite slow-motion of waterborne conveyances, of mingled fragrances of salt sea air, gutted fish, and marine exhaust, of the white noise of outboard engines, flapping sails, and myriad salutations—is a collage that earns the picturesque harbor its adjective.

The harbor is located at the midpoint of the town's shoreline and divides the beachfront neighborhoods into two roughly equal halves. Our neighborhood was in the west half. Our favorite beach there was Silver Beach, the bullies' preferred field of battle.

In summertime, when Charlie, Pudgy, and I were not playing baseball or football, or throwing anything we could get our hands on, we were swimming. Most often we went to Silver Beach. It was clean, popular with the girls, and only a half-hour's walk from our homes—half that if we rode our bikes.

We were allowed to go to Silver Beach by ourselves, provided we stuck together and never went into the water alone.

The tide was gentle at Silver Beach. It ebbed and flowed slowly, owing to a flat ocean floor extending out from the shore more than a hundred yards, exposing large sandbars at low tide. At high tide, the water was never more than shoulder-deep for at least those hundred yards, and we had strict orders not to venture out further than that unattended. These particular orders were not arbitrary and we were smart enough to obey them. But our difficulties with the bullies were never far from our mind, so we kept a very close watch out for them, and moved away smartly if they came into view.

We spent many happy hours at Silver Beach and learned to swim like fishes. As a consequence of our vigilance there, we learned that the bullies could not.

But swimming ability was not an element of their plan, that's why they preferred Silver Beach. It would be *good for them, bad for us.*

The plot thickens.

49

BUT WE DIDN'T NEED Sun Tzu to tell us to pick a venue *good for us, bad for them*. That's why we chose Gulf Beach.

Gulf Beach began at the mouth of the harbor and extended away easterly, for several hundred yards. We rarely went there because the beaches on our side of the harbor were closer and the sand was smoother. We were, however, sufficiently familiar with the layout of Gulf Beach, and—more to the point—the steepness of its shoreline, to find it ideal for our purposes.

Moreover, it was on the other side of the harbor, in the east half of town, inconveniently far away by our standards.

Getting to Gulf Beach from our neighborhood was not a simple proposition, even for adults. The harbor extended well into the center of town and there were no bridges across it. A virtual circumnavigation of the harbor was required to get to there, a circuitous route into and through the busy downtown business district, then down towards the eastern shore along an interminably long thoroughfare, appropriately named Gulf Street. On foot, this trip could take us kids at least two hours. There were buses, but none went directly from our neighborhood to Gulf Beach. Besides, we just didn't take busses; that cost money. When we got our hands on a nickel or a dime, we spent it on candy, not on bus fare. Feet or bicycles were our only modes of transportation. But in this particular case, bicycles were out. Parents in our neighborhood considered Gulf Beach the other side of the planet, and forbade biking there. Not even Socket Hair would risk a whipping if discovered biking all the way to the other side of the planet. So that left feet as the default mode of transportation. And since Socket Hair and Iggy-Piggy were so blindly determined to have it out with us, we were betting they would discount the travel time and hoof it across town, regardless of any consequences, which they assumed would be none.

That's another reason we chose Gulf Beach.

50

AT 4:00 PM THE NEXT DAY, Charlie, Pudgy, and I stood barefoot in the warm sand at Gulf Beach waiting for Billy and Iggy-Piggy. It was the first week of September, and the day was balmy as July. The sun shone brightly in a cloudless sky, and the water was still plenty warm enough for swimming. *Indian Summer*, they called it.

We stood idly in the center of the beach, a few yards from the water's edge, our backs to the water, wearing bathing suits and nothing else. Our only weapons were the famous facial expressions known euphemistically as shit-eating grins.

They appeared a few minutes later, trudging down the long hot road from town, sweating in the lingering rays of the afternoon sun. They had walked the entire way from our neighborhood, through the town center, around the harbor, and down Gulf Street, just as we expected they would.

Charlie lit up a broad grin and waved to them. "Over here, freakos," he yelled.

They spotted us and their spirits lifted. They started trotting slowly, in our direction, bellowing a string of off-color invectives, oblivious to sunbathers who were amused and to families who were not.

They were fully clothed, and did not appear to be carrying anything resembling weapons, although one never knew what could be concealed beneath their ragged garments. I wasn't concerned. I figured they were just so confident they could whip us with hands and fists that they had no need for arms. Besides, according to my plan, they'd be stripped down and in the water in a few minutes and then we'd know for sure.

So we stood, and watched in cautious fascination.

They came on, snarling and waving balled fists in menacing gestures.

As they drew closer, we could see that their appearance had not improved since the day we met them. It was as if they had never bathed or changed their clothes. Billy's hair was greasy as bacon fat and his clothes were, if not filthy, *filthier*. Iggy was resplendent in elfish green and red, grimace-smiling with a vacant stare, looking dumber than Mortimer Snerd. Piggy stunk liked a baked turd. A dip in the briny deep would improve their lot dramatically. They should thank us.

Then they eased their slow trot to a poor imitation of a John Wayne swagger. It was a lame attempt to tease out a dramatic build-up to a quick victory their pea-brains were already celebrating. Sunbathers now laughed openly at the pathetic spectacle. Families moved to quieter spots.

As they came to within ten yards of us, we drifted backwards, maintaining the separation, until they stood at the edge of the water and we stood in it, knee-deep, grinning at them. Pudgy blew kisses, and Charlie gave them a raspberry. Billy gave us a disgusted *okay-if-that's-the-way-you-wanna-play-it* look, turned on his heel, and led his minions back up the sand a few yards. They stripped down to their shorts and sat down.

When they were down, we came out of the water and stood on the sand again. Pudgy resumed taunting them, this time flapping his arms and making chicken sounds, "buk, buk, buk."

Charlie gave them another raspberry, a wet one, motioned *kiss-me* to Billy, and blew slobber in his direction.

I watched their eyes to gauge their next move; it was a rather futile exercise, not unlike staring into empty rooms.

They continued sitting in the sand, motionless, confused. They were probably waiting to see what we would do next. It was hard to tell with them.

We did nothing next. We just stood there.

Then I yelled at them in my best mocking tone, "Hello girls. Anyone coming out to play?"

Nothing.

After a short period of nobody doing anything, Billy looked up—or awakened, it wasn't clear which—leaned over, and conferred for a minute with Iggy-Piggy. Then they nodded to each other proudly as if they had found a prime number, and sat for another minute resting from the strenuous bout of thinking.

Finally, they lurched to their feet and ran straight for us as if we were not smart enough to anticipate a fast attack. Their hands were balled in fists again, and their faces were reddened with zeal. We jumped back into the water and drifted out slightly deeper. They plunged into the water after us, recklessly, slashing and flailing, until Billy and Iggy realized they were in waist-deep, Piggy realized he was in chest-deep, and they all realized it was getting deeper. Somewhat perplexed, they stopped abruptly, stood dumbly, and reassessed their situation.

After experimenting with more cautious movements, they got comfortable with the depth of the water, regained their confidence, and resumed the chase.

As a group, we moved laterally along the beach.

Soon they got cocky and tried to close on us.

Then we slid into chest-deep water.

This depth diminished Piggy's enthusiasm greatly, but not Billy's and Iggy's. They adjusted and clambered after us again.

We maintained this ploy until we identified a depth none of them were unwilling to exceed. From beyond that depth, we taunted them with catcalls and jeers, then we drifted back into shallower water and rekindled their enthusiasm with more taunts. They came after us again and we slipped back into the deeper water again. In this fashion, we settled into an endless game of cat-and-mouse.

They were blissfully unaware that while we had been pulling them *into* the water, we had also been pulling them *along* the shoreline, laterally, to our left, their right, towards the point where Gulf Beach merged with the wide-mouthed approach to the harbor. Cleverly, we had controlled the pace and direction of the chase, holding them at tantalizing distances for a specific length of time, while not revealing either our true swimming ability or the exact location to which the chase was headed.

51

THE SHORT NARROW CHANNEL—the spout of the funnel—is wide enough to allow boats to pass each other going and coming. There is no other access to the harbor so all traffic between the harbor and Long Island Sound must transit this channel.

At low tides, the width of the channel can shrink to less than a hundred yards at its narrowest point. During the *lowest* tides, the width of the channel can be too narrow for boats to pass each other, requiring them to stack up both inside and outside of the harbor, waiting their turn to transit, like cars taking turns on a one-lane bridge.

Sometimes, depending on the time of day, things are slow, and there is no traffic in the channel, or any approaching it, for many minutes.

And sometimes, depending on the moon, the stars, or the gods, the current is so powerful in the channel that only motor-driven craft are able to negotiate it.

It is a tricky channel.

There is no traffic *across* the channel *ever*, for this would not only be pointless, it would be foolhardy.

There is a strategic spot on the eastern side of this channel, to which we were now all headed.

Charlie, Pudgy and I continued falling back, in mock retreat, pulling Billy and Iggy-Piggy into the funnel. Billy was so passionately absorbed in the hunt, he did not realize, or did not care, that the cat-and-mouse exercise had dragged our melee past where the beach merged with the mouth of the harbor and into the channel. Apparently, he was unconcerned with this development, figuring he would chase us into the harbor, and all round it, if he had to. He seemed similarly unconcerned that the chase had taken quite a long time and the beautiful sunset now unfolding was soon to be followed by that uncompromising time of day when darkness falls and little kids must be home in their houses, on pain of death or spanking.

Eventually we arrived at our destination, the strategic spot on the eastern side of the channel, a spit of sandy shore that sloped steeply into it. Our neighborhood on the west side of town was less than a hundred yards from this spot, straight across the channel, separated only by a dying tidal current ebbing gently out of the harbor. Our choice of meeting at Gulf Beach was designed to bring us all to this place, at this moment in time. So far, our plan was working nicely, owing to our research and study.

52

THE STARTING POINTS of our research had been the legions of old duffers hanging around the harbor, swapping sea stories, tinkering with boats, and fishing from docks and piers. We spent hours discussing tides and traffic with those who would indulge us. We approached each old duffer with good manners and feigned innocence. We did not feign sincerity, however, that part was real.

Not every old man was taken with us. Some were just grumpy old buzzards who had no time for children as it distracted them from the business at hand. Some were neither grumpy nor helpful, just tired, operating at the limits of their concentration, unable or unwilling to depart from routine. But we kept at it, groveled politely, and found the rare ones, like Otto, who were proud to share their knowledge, and appreciative of kids who were eager to soak it up. These were the ones had who taught us how to use the tide charts—we could read, after all—from which we had figured out when the tide would be low and the channel narrow. These were the ones who had explained the traffic patterns in the harbor and identified the time of day—between 5:00 and 6:00 PM—when the fewest boats transited the channel.

While Billy and Iggy-Piggy had been focusing blindly on the chase, I had been secretly monitoring the status of traffic in and out of the harbor. And I had been manipulating the speed of the chase so that we would arrive at this strategic spot on the channel when there was no traffic in it, or any approaching.

Charlie, Pudgy, and I stopped abruptly at the strategic spot. The chase was over; the enemies just didn't know it yet.

We stood in the water, chest-deep, facing the shore, backs to the channel, and allowed Billy and Iggy-Piggy to believe they could advance to within striking distance of us.

By now, they were red-hot with emotion, unable to hide expressions that screamed wordlessly, "At last! At last!"

They could taste victory. They could feel it. They were blinded by it—once again. We counted on that.

They charged into the water blindly, waving their balled fists high in the air hysterically, anticipating sweet contact with our grinning faces.

Billy led the charge. He came straight at me. His raging fists, so long denied, descended swiftly, mightily, accurately.

Whiff.

Splash.

"Goddammit!" screamed Billy.

Nothing but water.

I was gone.

Within a hair's breadth of being struck, I had melted backwards—into the channel.

Charlie and Pudgy did the same.

The sandy bottom fell off abruptly. Piggy sensed it first, scrambled backwards, and managed to keep his feet on solid ground. Iggy was between Piggy and Billy and also managed to keep his feet on solid ground. But Billy had been too impulsive. Having led the charge, he was farthest out. The bottom disappeared under him. He yelped in fright, and sank. His feet churned and his arms thrashed as he fought to stay afloat and regain his footing. Iggy reached out, grabbed an arm, and pulled him back.

The three of them thrashed and flailed and finally scrambled up onto dry land and flopped down in the sand, gasping for air.

After a few minutes they were able to stand and take stock of the situation. They watched in stunned silence, mouths agape in puzzlement—watched Charlie, Pudgy, and me swim away, across the channel.

No one *ever* swam *across* the channel.

Charlie, Pudgy, and I were like Bre'er Rabbit in the briar patch. We had swum across the channel before. Several times. Earlier in the day, we swam across it to get to Gulf Beach. Now we were swimming back. Piece of cake.

Upon leaving Billy and Iggy-Piggy flapping in the water on the east side of the channel, we had set out easily across it, employing the most basic swimming stroke, the Australian Crawl. A monkey can do it.

We angled our direction slightly, to the right, and rode the mildly ebbing current in a wide arc back around towards the left, where it deposited us onto a tiny patch of dry land that marked the end of the beach road, next to the little dock belonging to the Milford Yacht Club. The old duffers had explained how a current can be an enemy if you *oppose* it and a friend if you go *with* it. And they were right.

Emerging from the water, we shook ourselves off and danced a little jig of triumph on the tiny patch of dry land. Then we whirled about and saluted our enemies on the opposite shore. They were still standing there, open-mouthed, unsure of what they had just seen. Soon, they would wake up and realize, all too late, that they had been out-foxed again, and now they had a long walk home ahead of them. But first, they would have to back-track to Gulf Beach, find their clothes, and only then could they begin the long trek home. Then perhaps they would remember, all too late, that it was the first week of September—when darkness falls earlier than mid-summer—and it would be full dark by the time they got home. And now they were in a world of hurt.

Otto had advised that we shouldn't *engage* them.

And so, we hadn't.

Maybe we *provoked* them a little.

We retrieved our clothes and bicycles from a growth of bushes next to the dock, got dressed, and headed home.

We passed the neighborhood pharmacy, in front of which was a pay phone, and Pudgy yelled, "Whoa, whoa, wait a minute, guys, I got an idea."

We stopped.

"What idea?" said Charlie.

"Let's call Billy's mother, and rat him out?"

"Are you crazy? I said. "That's a little reckless. You're forgetting, she's some kinda witch or something. She might put a spell or a curse on us if she finds out the truth." I had visions of the phone call interrupting a coven or a sacrifice or a boiling of roots, arousing her ire, inspiring the deployment of witchcraft in our direction.

Pudgy was quick to respond, "It's a little too late to worry about *reckless*, after what we just did. I ain't worried. If you're chicken, I'll do it."

"I ain't chicken," I said, employing the three words required of any red-blooded American boy in such instance.

"Me neither," said Charlie, equally red-blooded.

"But since it's your idea, go ahead," I said magnanimously.

So he did.

"Hello, Mrs. O'Reilly, this is Pudgy Tookis. I just saw Billy at Gulf Beach, fighting with some smaller kids."

Click.

We were home in fifteen minutes, before it got dark.

53

WE NEVER TOLD OUR PARENTS we routinely swam across the harbor. If they ever found out, we would be in far greater trouble than Billy O'Reilly and Iggy-Piggy. Not getting home before dark was a minor infraction compared to the trouble we would be in. We might even be in jail. Surely there was a maritime law against swimming across an active harbor channel. I thought about that once or twice, but it interfered with the shortest-distance-between-two-points-is-a-straight-line theory, so I put it away in a corner of my brain, for safe keeping.

In truth, however, a minor interference with a specious theory cannot fully explain our foolhardiness. No, a more compelling explanation is simply that we were *boys*, and boys are indestructible. The simplest explanation is the most accurate, when it's right before your nose.

Indestructibility is a mindset, another facet of the insidious testosterone curse. It compels us to act before we think. It's not our fault. It's how we are built. Our pain receptors, like sweat glands, do not develop until after adolescence. And then their progress is unfairly slow. Consider the following illustration, a birthday party for a girl of six or seven, in which boys are invited: The girls will sit, they will talk, they will laugh, they will sing, they will dance, they will eat and drink properly, and they will comport themselves with civility and grace, without damaging their surroundings, while the opposite is true of boys. We will rage about with reckless abandon, we will scream and yell, we will fight, we will throw food, we will break dishes, abuse pets, and careen off walls, doors, and furniture without sensation of pain or discomfort, our pain transmission system undeveloped and not fully functional. Therein lay the problem. It is unclear which mechanism is the culprit. Are the nerve endings, the nociceptors, not sensing pressure or deformation yet? Is the message not getting through to the spinal cord and thence to the brain yet? Is the thalamus, deep inside the brain, not sending an *ouch* yet? We don't know. What we do know is that our pain transmission system works eventually. So the logical conclusion is that it develops at a slower rate than it does in girls.

In early childhood, as the illustration demonstrates, boys develop without the full benefit of pain or discomfort. That leaves us bereft of tools to evaluate the consequences of anti-social behavior. Without such consequences, we are left with the erroneous conclusion that we are indestructible, hence the mindset. Thus we are saddled with another imperfection. It is the lot of boys.

Usually the mindset moderates by the age of forty, and eventually fades away. Then, when we are very old and it's gone completely, we wonder how we could have been so stupid in the first place. *That* is the lot of men.

Or maybe it's a whole lot simpler than all of that. Boys are just plain dumber than girls. Janie and Mary Lou could swim just as well as we could, but you wouldn't see them swimming across no harbor. No sir, you wouldn't.

54

I COULD HARDLY WAIT to tell Otto how I had finally taken his advice. Family matters and a school fair kept me busy for a few days, so I wasn't able to get over to Lacey's Golf Range until Saturday.

A stranger with a sad face was sitting at the counter reading a newspaper when I approached. It was just after 10:00 AM, and there were no customers yet.

"Excuse me, Sir. I'm looking for Otto," I said, in the formal address Otto had taught me to use with adults and strangers.

"He died," the stranger said, as calmly as if he hadn't.

"What?" I said softly, forgetting my manners.

"He died," the stranger repeated.

I froze in place; stood stock-still for a minute, unable to breath. My brain was not quite processing what I just heard. Then it did. And it hit me like a punch in the face.

"What?" I squawked, not caring about manners. "He can't be dead. I saw him right here, just the other day."

"He died two days ago. Some kinda cancer. Sorry kid."

"No, no, no! He can't be dead!" I bawled. "He can't! He can't! He can't!"

My brain began more processing, and my legs turned to rubber. I sank to the floor. My chest heaved and hot tears burned trails down my cheeks. I sat dumbfounded for a few minutes, not knowing what to say or do. A car pulled into the parking lot and two customers got out with golf clubs in their hands, joking with each other. I despised them their insensitivity. I despised the stranger with the sad face for telling me Otto died. I despised everybody who was driving by on the Boston Post Road because they were alive and Otto was not.

I scurried away before the two customers could see me. I thought about a place to hide. I was confused. I wandered over to Otto's ancient tractor, sitting silently in the yard by the maintenance shed, climbed into the driver's seat that usually smelled like gasoline but this time smelled like Otto, and cried some more.

There seemed to be a hole in my world, a giant vacuum. Where once there was a kindness and a friendship, communication and acknowledgement, there would be nothing. Gone. No explanation. No good bye. Just gone.

I sat in the ancient tractor and thought about the hours and hours David B Lacey and I, and sometimes even Pudgy and Charlie, had sat in the maintenance shed mesmerized by Otto's stories. I thought about the several lifetimes Otto had lived before he ever came to Lacey's Golf Range, where he developed a tic from sitting in this very same seat. Soon a dam burst, and a thousand recollections flowed like a fast-moving river, continuous and homogenous like the molecules of the water, becoming a single unbroken recollection, replacing my tears. There was Otto explaining how he grew up in rural Mississippi with a colored kid named Alby, who was his best friend but couldn't go to the same school or pee in the same toilet so they would save up and pee together in the river, and it seemed to Otto that Alby's unfair childhood was just preparation for the day as an adult when he was lynched by three white men for helping a white lady fix a broken pump handle, and Otto left Mississippi the very next day and went to Florida and picked oranges for several years. And in 1898 when he was twenty-eight years old he submitted an application, along with thousands of other men who were called patriots, to join Teddy Roosevelt's Rough Riders and fight the Spanish in Cuba, and only 560 men were chosen and he wasn't one of them. And in 1915 he volunteered for service in the first World War, and put his age down as thirty-five when he was really forty-five, and was accepted and sent to France where he was a stretcher bearer at the 2nd Battle of the

Marne River in 1918, and got shot in the leg—but not badly. And while there, he met and fell in love with a French woman named Cherise, and promised to come back for her after the war, but when he finally saved enough money it was a couple years later and he could hardly remember what she looked like, and the memory faded and he never went back. And Charlie was with us this time, and asked Otto if he had a scar on his leg from getting shot, and Otto said "yes," and Charlie asked if we could see it, and Otto said "yes," but he could not show it by rolling up his pant-leg because the scar was high up on his right thigh, so he unbuckled his belt and lowered his pants and showed us, and Charlie asked if he could touch it, and Otto said "no, take a quick look," and immediately pulled up his pants, saying that if anybody came by and saw him with his pants down in a shed with a bunch of kids they would surely get the wrong impression, and he thought that was very funny and laughed so hard that tears came to his eyes. And then he worked for ten years up and down the East Coast at various unskilled and unsatisfying jobs, but he kept his sanity by pulling practical jokes because he said "life without jokes was like a cake without icing," and when I asked him to tell about a gag he pulled he said, one time he worked in an office pool, and the day before Christmas everyone went to lunch at a bar and had a few drinks to celebrate the holidays, and while they were out he put a big goldfish in the glass water cooler, and when they came back to the office to punch out and go home early, some of them went to the water cooler and got a cup of water to clear their palettes and were drinking it when they saw the goldfish swimming around and weren't sure what they were seeing because they were a little tipsy, and all the while he was standing in the background laughing his ass off. And that reminded him that we should promise not to tell our parents that he taught us swear words like "piss" and "shit" and "bastard." And when he was working on the docks in Brooklyn, New York unloading fruit and vegetables, the stock market crashed—whatever that meant—and he got fired so he joined a company of mercenary soldiers, because it was the only job he could find even though he was fifty-nine at the time, but because he had been in the Army and knew how to handle a gun and was tough as nails from heaving fruit and vegetables around on the docks, the mercs were glad to have him. They called him Pops and sent him somewhere in the middle of Africa where he was posted with a ragtag unit whose mission was to slaughter a whole village including women and children, and he wanted no part of it so he and a guy named Eddie who had become his best friend ran away. A few months later, they ended up in a place called Nairobi in eastern Africa where Eddie got Malaria and was bedridden for three months. Otto and a native lady named Ngina, who was a Kikuyu and daughter of the tribe's chief, nursed Eddie back to health. Otto and Ngina fell in love during those months caring for Eddie, and Otto had to give the chief ten goats and five cows for permission to marry her, and they were very happy for a year but she died giving birth to a daughter, who also died, so he decided to come home. When Eddie was well enough to travel, they left Nairobi together in 1931. Eddie's last name was Lacey, and he was David B Lacey's grandfather, and he had inherited ten acres of land on the Boston Post Road in a small town Otto had never heard of, called Milford, in the state of Connecticut Otto had never been to, so that's where they headed. And when they saw the land, Eddie Lacey got the idea for Lacey's Golf Range, and together they built the business, but Otto never had a piece of the action because something in the deed to the land prohibited it. But Eddie never forgot that Otto had saved him from dying of Malaria in Africa, and so Eddie treated him like a brother and gave him lifetime use of the cottage behind the big house, where he still lived, and for the first time in his life he had a home and job he was proud of. The next ten years were the happiest of his life, and then the Japanese bombed Pearl Harbor and he was so mad that he wished he was young enough to join the army and kill a thousand Japs, but when the Enola Gaye dropped an atom bomb on a city called Hiroshima and incinerated thousands of them in the blink of an eye, he cried like a baby. And he hated Adolph Hitler and called him a fairy, and loved Winston Churchill and called him Winnie, and he was ambivalent about Franklin Roosevelt even though he was Teddy's fifth cousin, and he had loved Harry Truman until he dropped the A-bombs. After the war Eddie retired and his son, who was David B's father, took over the business and Otto continued working as if nothing happened, and he hoped that some day David B would take over the business and carry it on. And although Eddie was no longer involved in day-to-day operations, he was still active and gave advice from time to time, and they were still best friends and they played chess regularly up at the big house. And one day recently, one of his friends turned seventy-five, and for his birthday Otto invited him to come by and hit out a few balls on-the-house, and he slipped a gag ball into the bucket and his friend was having a delightful time whacking out balls when the gag ball exploded with a bigger bang than he expected, and it startled his friend so badly that the friend almost croaked on the spot. It startled Otto too and he was ashamed of himself because it was supposed to be a harmless practical joke and instead it turned out to be a dirty trick, and so he had to take the old guy to the nearest bar and fortify him with scotch and apologies to repair their friendship, and he laughed after telling this story because he had called his friend the old guy, and the old guy was actually five years younger than him, and we were all laughing at this story—

David B Lacey tapped me on the shoulder and I woke up. I guess I had dozed off from emotional exhaustion. I blinked and looked around to see where I was, and my head started to clear. Then I remembered what I had been dreaming about, and it gave me enough strength to face David B without balling again.

David B said, "He had cancer, but didn't tell anybody, except my grandfather. Didn't want anybody to fret. Pretty tough guy. I'm sure gonna miss him. There's a funeral tomorrow, if you wanna come."

I didn't respond immediately. I was still a little groggy. After a few moments, I said, "Are you going?"

"Yeah, I have to."

"Does that mean you don't *want* to?" I said.

"Nah, I didn't mean it that way. I wanna go. He was like another grandfather. I loved him."

"I loved him to, I guess, when you put it that way. But I don't think I can do it. I wanna just remember him alive. Thanks anyway."

55

I WALKED HOME IN A DAZE. I had not exhausted my recollections of Otto, but I had exhausted my emotional self. My head was downcast as if I was guilty of some egregious trespass. I kicked at stones in the road as I walked. I didn't want to talk to anybody and I didn't want anybody to talk to me.

And then, out of nowhere, there he was, standing right in front of me, blocking my way, waiting to be noticed—Socket Hair Billy O'Reilly.

Momentarily startled, I stopped short and looked up. He was his usual rancid self. A couple of flies buzzed around his oily red hair, as if they had left Charlie's shoes for better hunting grounds. It made me sick.

"You guys think you're so smart," he said, maliciously.

For whatever he was planning, he could not have had worse timing. We were both alone, so it was just the two of us. I was not scared. On the contrary, I was so wired with tension from the events of the day that I believed—if pushed too far—I would tear him apart like a rabid dog.

He shifted his stance imperceptibly, attempted a posture of intimidation, and babbled an incoherent challenge, containing words that sounded like *dare* and *alone* and *chicken* that I barely heard and only partially assimilated because I was seething with anger and righteousness.

A low feral growl began to emanate from somewhere within my core, and it startled me as much as it did him. My eyes were already red from crying, and they took on a luminous cast as I began fuming and hyper-ventilating and writhing like a coiled snake.

My first thought was to jump on his face and rip his lips off, and my agitation must have conveyed that thought because he took a small step backwards and hesitated from doing whatever he had planned to do next.

My second thought, from the lessons of Otto, overrode my first thought. I would not engage him, at least not in combat. But this insight did not diminish my rage.

With the violence of an animal backed into a corner, I spring forward and pushed him in the chest. Madness flashed in my eyes, propelled me forward, and I pushed him again and again. He stumbled backward and tripped and fell on his ass. I stood over him, and this time, it was I who brandished a balled fist. I bent over and held the fist an inch from his face. I was trembling, my fist was trembling, and I screamed in his ear, **"Are you so goddamn stupid you can't see messing with Pudgy and Charlie and me is a waste of time? We don't wanna fight. If you force us to, we will hurt you bad. Stay … away … from … us!"**

I walked away.

He sat up, ashen-faced, and wiped my spittle from his face. That was the last of our troubles with Billy O'Reilly and Iggy-Piggy.

Otto would be proud.

56

NOBODY BOTHERED ME the next week. Otto's passing had left a somber pall hanging over me and I kept to myself until the following Monday.

I found Charlie and Pudgy at the usual place down at the creek. They were sitting quietly, contemplating the blackened remains of something, probably tadpoles. I told them about my confrontation with Billy O'Reilly and that I guessed we wouldn't have any more trouble from him and Iggy-Piggy. They both nodded softly but didn't offer anything in response.

We sat quietly for a few minutes, all three of us contemplating the blackened remains now. Finally, I said, "You know guys, everywhere I go I see Otto. Not that that's a bad thing, it feels good to remember him. But I need to get my mind on something else—something cheery."

"The snake gag," said Charlie.

"Oh, that's cheery," I said.

"Well, you thought it was cheery once."

"Yeah," added Pudgy. "You've been avoiding it all summer. It's like you're chicken or something."

The C word is hard for a boy to back away from.

"Okay, you got me. That's not a bad idea. I'll do it tomorrow. Honest."

The next day after school, Charlie and Pudgy were on me like green on parsley.

"Let's go, Houdini," from Charlie.

"Let's go, Tarzan," from Pudgy.
No preamble, just naked challenge.
"All right, all right," I said, knowing this was it.
Once again we headed to the Field. I still had some trepidation; but this time I had tad of motivation, an attribute new to the equation. It helped a little. But only a little.

Since I had the obligation to lead the way, I took the route around the block so we would not pass Janie's house. This was a precaution, just in case I wasn't able to find a snake again.

The sun shone brightly; there were few clouds in the sky. And there was no football game in progress at the little park by the Field to disturb its quietude or disperse its snakes. My lucky day.

I rummaged around in the tall grass, and located the forked stick I had teased more times than God teased Job. I picked it up, tested its heft, and commenced the hunt.

Charlie and Pudgy complained that this was getting old, but no amount of complaining diminished their work ethic. They went to opposite sides of the Field like seasoned trackers—which they were by now—and began to thrash the tall grass towards the middle, where I was poised with the forked stick.

After an hour or so of honest searching, it seemed like the day would be another bust. I was hot and thirsty, and having my usual second thoughts about holding a snake, when Charlie yelled, "There's one, there's one, over here, hurry up."

Pudgy and I converged on Charlie who was pointing down at a real live snake slithering through the grass. I shuddered, shivered, quivered, and shook, all in a split second.

Finally, I mustered enough courage to pin the beast down with the forked stick. He twisted angrily. No big deal. The stick was five feet long. It took an hour, or so it seemed, to work my way down the stick to the snake. No hurry. Then the moment of truth, time to do the unthinkable—touch it. That took another hour, again so it seemed, and yet another to grasp it behind the head.

Finally, there, got it.

Shuddering, I picked it up.

"Oh jeez, jeez, jeez, holy crap, holy crap," I blubbered for composure, as it wrapped itself around my arm. I fought off a bowel movement and held fast.

Eventually, I gained my composure and stood erect. I held the prize aloft triumphantly, like Perseus holding the head of Medusa.

Hero.

Champion.

Cocky now, I thrust it tauntingly towards Charlie and Pudgy. Charlie backed up a step, worshipful, hacked up something yellow, and made obeisance. Pudgy fell down and rolled away like a snowball down a steep hill—an extraordinary feat for a fat kid on level ground.

But I had done it.

I was *holding* a snake.

I was delirious with power, and I proclaimed myself King of the World.

57

WITH A MIGHTY SERPENT entwined about my arm, I led a triumphal march through the streets of the neighborhood to my house. A ragged urchin and a florid preppy comprised my retinue. Charlie bounced like a pogo stick and Pudgy waddled like a duck, both a respectful distance behind, basking in the glow of complicity.

Crowds lined the streets, cheering wildly.

John Souza music filled the air.

Flaxen-haired maidens threw kisses and petals of rose from gilded balconies.

Silver horns heralded my passage.

Janie applauded loudly, enthusiastically.

Mary Lou thrust her butt in my direction and beamed adoringly—at least in my mind's eye.

Tweedle Dee and Tweedle Dum burst through the crowd, and broadcast encouragement through a new gizmo.

I waved the snake at them in acknowledgment.

Countess Fensterwald stood on the sidewalk, holding a new white poodle protectively, pointing at Charlie as if she were identifying him for the police. An image appeared over her shoulder, part of a face, indistinct, as in a fog, eyes questioning, Otto perhaps, lasting brief seconds if at all, and then dissolved. I felt it more than saw it.

Billy O'Reilly stood behind the crowd, hiding sheepishly, convinced at last that he should never, ever again, mess with the crazy kid who fondles snakes.

I could feel his surrender.

Iggy Plickett sat on the curb in a new elf outfit, trying to force a smile out of his crowded mouth.

Piggy was nowhere to be seen but a foul stench suggested he was hiding behind Iggy.

Yubie trailed after us, huffing, clanking, waving a baseball bat, shouting, "On Yubang," in my honor, making it a universal entreaty.

It was proof.

I was the great and powerful Oz..

I was King of the World.

I was also hallucinating wildly, not from the adoration of the crowd but from the rush of adrenalin that comes naturally to any sane person holding a snake.

But I was focused on the objective nevertheless.

Victory was near.

58

WE REACHED MY HOUSE and went around to the back door. My mother was at the kitchen sink with her back to me. She didn't suspect a thing.

I sneaked in the back door, unnoticed.

I looked over my shoulder at Charlie and Pudgy to make sure I had an audience. They stepped quietly inside the door behind me.

Pudgy was in high anticipation. He wore a sadistic grin I'd not seen before, but confirmed my suspicion that he got his nut pulling wings off his butterflies.

Charlie was trancelike, foaming at the mouth. His skinny little frame gestured frantically, *do it, do it.* He was so excited, he had *no* good eye; two Tasmanian devils whirled around inside their sockets trying to leap free.

Janie and Mary Lou had followed along and were outside watching from a cautious distance. Their expressions were more abstract than curious.

Time at last.

This would be sweet.

"Hey Ma, look."

She turned around and I flipped her the snake.

Time stood still.

We waited for the kind of shriek a startled mother makes upon seeing a mouse.

Nothing.

We waited for the mother of all shrieks a mother *should* make when flipped a snake.

Nothing.

She caught it like we were a circus act.

"Oh cute," she said, holding it comfortably like a kitten. "My brother used to do this to me all the time."

Then she smiled kindly, and suffused in a halo of motherly wisdom, flipped the thing back at me.

"AAAAAGGHH!" I shrieked.

The composure I had gained in minute increments over long hours of concentration shattered instantly like dropped crystal.

The false bravado I had affected to accompany my fragile composure was naked without it and evaporated with it.

A fiery dragon loosed from the bowels of Hell arched through the air at me.

The beast was twenty feet long and two feet thick.

It was black and blue and green and red and yellow.

It roared, rotated, pulsated, twisted and turned.

Its eyes were opalescent saucers that pierced mine like arrows.

It hated me.

It wanted to kill me.

Its cavernous mouth snapped open to engulf my head, and an immense forked tongue spat bolts of orange fire at me through glistening golden fangs.

It bellowed a mighty roar that sounded like my name.

Its breath stunk of puke and swamp and liver.

It landed on my chest, writhing angrily, and went for my heart.

"AAAAAGGHH!" I shrieked again.

My head spun like a top and my sphincter rippled like a whoopie cushion.

I whirled around and leapt for the door.

The snake fell to the floor.

Charlie and Pudgy freaked too, started shrieking, and made for the door.

Three Stooges jammed the doorway at the same instant—***whooboop-whoop-whoop***—and there, for the longest second of my young life, ensued a world-class scrum—***whoob-oop-whoop-whoop***—then we tumbled out into the yard—***whoob-oop-whoop-whoop***—and the three of us hit the ground running as if chased by bears.

59

IT HAD BEEN a seminal summer. I had grown two inches, made new friends, learned hard truths, and won great victories. I was full of myself. I thought I could pull off one more victory without breaking a sweat. I thought I could outwit my mother.

So I had tried. But now Janie and Mary Lou were rolling on the lawn howling with laughter and I was running down the street with Charlie and Pudgy.

I imagined what Otto would've said: "Nice goin', Sonny Boy. That was a beauty, that was. You were doin' fine all summer, then you hadda be a hotshot."

Charlie and Pudgy stopped after a block or so and sat down on the curb to catch their breath. I kept on alone for a bit, needing to reflect on the imagined rebuke.

I slowed down to a contemplative stroll, called back, "I'll see you guys later," and thought hard about the last few minutes and the next order of business. Should I consider the gag a humiliation? Should I try to redeem myself with another gag? Indeed, do I *need* to redeem myself? If so, what—if anything—would I gain? Rekindled pride? Bogus flattery? On the other hand, if I accept the event as enlightenment, if I count it a proper lesson and nothing more, if I shrug it off and move on, would that not *be* a great victory?

I was on my own now. There was no more Otto to prop me up. I had to reach my own conclusions, make my own decisions, walk in my own shoes.

I turned back and chased after Charlie and Pudgy, who had gotten to their feet and were trudging off towards the Field.

"Anybody for football," I yelled at their backs.

978-0-595-44810-4
0-595-44810-0